AIDAN

HIGHLAND PASSAGES

ANNIS REID

AIDAN

Book Two of the *Highland Passages* Series!

Piper Kaminski's a bass player in a band that just got contract. So why is she poking around a group of rocks that remind her of Stonehenge? Why? Because Piper's lead singer and her odd but hunky boyfriend are skulking around the henge and looking for something.

Piper's a take-action kind of girl. So she's going to find out what they're doing. She trails them to the henge. But in the middle of the night, she finds herself confronted with an unconscious hottie. When he comes to, she's got all kinds of problems because he acts like he's never seen cars. Or jeans. Or anything in this century.

He's at her mercy it would seem. Except her heart appears to be in his mercy.

When she realizes that Aidan knows her lead singer's boyfriend, pieces of a strange puzzle start to fall into place.

1

"I feel like I'm walking on air. I never could've imagined it being that great!" Piper couldn't keep still after what was probably one of the greatest sets of her life. Even if it was only two songs long.

"Careful," Jimmy warned as he poured himself another shot. "You might take flight if you don't calm down."

"I might take flight?" She smirked, lifting the bottle of Scotch, noting how light it was. "This was full when we got here today. Don't start making fun just because I'm excited that we kicked—"

"Okay, okay." Anna stepped between them and grabbed one of the shot glasses, lifting it to her mouth and bolting it back in a short, practiced gesture Piper rarely saw from her. She wasn't exactly a drinker; at least she didn't drink much in public.

Then again, she didn't seem much like herself at all. Practically a different person than she was just that morning, before the show, when they were setting up and going through sound check.

After the performance she had given and the way the audience reacted—it was such a rush, when they were really and truly connected with the music—she should've been relaxed and satisfied and maybe looking forward to the future.

Now? She was just as shaky and anxious as any of them had been before the set. Maybe more so.

"Are you doing okay?" Piper asked her, pulling her away from Jimmy and Ed. They were having a good time on their own, half-soused and determined to get all the way there. Celebrating, the way anybody would after they played so well.

But here was Anna, acting like she had just seen a ghost.

"I'm fine," she said with a shrug, but that was obviously a lie. Piper might have been much better with a bass than she was at... just about anything else, but she wasn't a dummy.

"Are you sure? You know you can tell me, right? Two chicks against the world."

That got a smile, anyway, even if it was the barest hint. "Two chicks against the world," she repeated in a whisper. "Yeah. Sometimes I forget."

"Does that mean you're gonna tell me what's going on with you? And why you got onstage looking different than you did this morning?"

That got a reaction, anyway. Anna's brows lifted practically off her forehead. "Oh. Right."

"I mentioned it earlier, but I think it bears repeating." Piper touched the part in her own bright-red locks, then pointed to Anna's head. She had a skunk stripe running through her black hair that hadn't been there in the morning. Piper would've bet every last cent she had on it.

That gig had been the biggest thing they'd ever done, hands down. No way would the meticulous, everything's-riding-on-this Anna have let her roots come in without dying them well in advance of the performance. She had a lot on her mind, but that wouldn't have slipped through.

Besides, Piper was completely sure she would've noticed it before. The girl's natural color was a very fair shade of blond, completely the opposite of what she dyed it. Not the sort of thing a person missed when they were standing under dozens of lights.

Anna looked away, toward somebody outside the tent. A beefy guy. Piper had noticed him before, just after their set, when Anna was talking quietly with him. Hot, for sure, but... weird. Like everything freaked him out. She wondered if he was on something. But it wasn't Anna's style to hang out with a guy who took drugs, either. Ever.

Besides, they weren't exactly familiar with the country. When did she have time to make a friend? Maybe he was a cosplayer from someplace near the amphitheater since he wore what Piper could only describe to herself as a costume—a loose shirt that hung halfway to his knees, belted at the waist. Tight pants. A plaid sash draped over his chest, tucked into the belt, hanging over his shoulder and down his back.

"Who's that guy?" she finally had to ask.

"Hmm?" Anna's head snapped back, away from his direction, her wide eyes focused on Piper. Was she guilty of something? She had that sort of look on her face. But what could she possibly have to feel guilty about?

"I asked you who the hottie is," Piper repeated with a grin. "You keep looking at him, you know."

"I do?"

"Yeah. Not that I blame you. The guys around here are so much hotter than the ones back home. They could learn a lesson." And she was always a sucker for a brogue.

The hottie looked into the tent, making eye contact with Piper before his gaze shifted over to Anna. He stared at her like she was the only person in the entire world. But it wasn't a romantic sort of look.

The guy looked scared. Like Anna was the only person who could help him. It was enough to make Piper wonder if the two of them had known each other before this. But no, Anna had never come to Scotland before they flew in together, just for the festival.

"Are you gonna introduce me?" Piper pressed on. Normally, she would've let it go, but something about this didn't sit right.

When Anna gaped at her like a deer in headlights. "Uh. Um. I don't know. I guess?"

"Now I'm more interested than ever," she teased. That was true. How was anybody supposed not to be interested in a mysterious, hunky Scot?

"We're supposed to be waiting here for those guys to meet up with us. From the record company." That was why they were waiting in the tent, to begin with, rather than enjoying the festival or going back to their hotel to decompress. They'd gotten word that a pair of executives wanted to talk to them and would they consider hanging around for a little bit for that meeting?

Who wouldn't?

Even so, that didn't mean they had to stand in the same spot until the guys showed up. "Sure, and we're only going over there to talk to your friend. Relax, would you? What's the big deal?"

"I don't know." Anna sighed. "Okay. Come on. I just wanna warn you, though. He's not very social."

"Okay." What a weird thing to say. What a completely weird situation, all the way around. What was Anna doing with this guy if he came with all these warnings and basically looked like he had been dropped into their world from another planet?

Anna reached him first and had the chance to murmur something to him before Piper caught up. "Kaden, this is Piper. She's the bassist for the band."

He nodded, smiling just a little. The guy was even better looking close-up. His jaw could cut glass. And his eyes were so intense, deep-set and hazel and sparkling with something that wasn't friendliness. "Aye, I recall seeing ye on the stage. Ye did verra well, lass."

She couldn't help it. He sounded like something out of a historical drama, which totally matched up with his costume. How was she supposed to not giggle a little at the thickness of his brogue? And the way he called her lass? Who did that anymore?

But it wasn't a joke. He wasn't playing. Her giggle died under the weight of his and Anna's stares. "Hi, Kaden. Thank you for the compliment." At least it sounded like a compliment. Was it?

Anna practically grimaced. "Okay. So. You've met. Uh, Kaden and I have some business we have to get to once we meet with the executives. That's why he's waiting here for me."

She and Kaden had business together? "What sort of business?" she couldn't help but ask. This was news to her, and the fact that it was happening now, after their make-or-break gig, only made her more suspicious than ever.

"It's a long story," Anna assured her, rolling her eyes. "And it's not that big a deal."

"I'm not doing anything else right now," Piper reminded her with a shrug. "And if it's no big deal, you can tell me about it. Right?"

Her smiled tightened. "Can I have a second with you?" She took Piper's wrist and pulled her aside, away from Kaden. "What's the big deal? Why are you acting like a detective all of a sudden?"

"Because you're acting like a criminal all of a sudden!" Piper hissed. "You've never mentioned this guy before just now, and we've barely spent more than a few minutes apart since we got to Scotland. When would you even have the chance to meet him? What sort of business could you have with him? Sorry if you're my friend and I don't want to think of you getting into anything dangerous or sketchy."

Anna sighed, her shoulders falling back into their normal position instead of hunched up around her ears. "Is that what you're worried about? Believe me, it's nothing sketchy. There's nothing you have to worry about."

"So why all the secrecy?"

"No offense, because I definitely see you as a friend, too, but I can't share every last thing with you. Trust me, it's just something I have to take care of. It won't take more than a few minutes, I'm sure. And it can wait until our meeting with the executives, too."

That was probably supposed to comfort her, but it didn't. If anything, she was left with more questions than before. Had Anna been lying the whole time? Did she already have connections or ties to Scotland that she had never spoken of? What would she have to gain by lying?

It was obvious she wouldn't get any straight answers if she came right out and ask for them, so Piper chose instead to smile and shrug it off. "Okay. I trust your judgment."

"Do you know whose judgment I don't trust?" Anna jogged over to the guys, who seemed to have a goal they were working toward; emptying that bottle of Jamison and probably making complete fools of themselves in front of executives who held the band's future in their hands.

Piper decided to take the chance and sidle back up to Kaden, who looked more and more out of place with each passing minute. People walked by dressed in normal, everyday clothes, making the difference starker all the time. "So, I guess you're from around here?" she asked, giving him the most genuine smile she could manage.

He nodded. "Aye."

A man of few words. "From Edinburgh?" She prompted, wondering if she could pry him out of his shell and find out how he was connected to Anna.

The timing was odd. That was what bothered her. Anna had never mentioned having so much as an acquaintance in Scotland, and now this guy stood by the tent like he was guarding her. Or like she was guarding him, and they couldn't be apart from each other.

A strange thought, but Piper couldn't seem to shake it.

He frowned, thick brows lowering over those intense eyes of his. "Nay, farther away than that." But he wouldn't offer any more information. If he was trying to give the impression of being a normal person, he was failing miserably.

"Piper!" Anna waved enthusiastically from inside the tent, and Piper noticed a pair of men in khakis and polo shirts shaking hands with Jimmy and Ed.

"I hope they can hold their liquor," she muttered, telling herself to forget this stranger for a few minutes in favor of doing what they had come to do.

But that didn't mean she would forget him completely. No way. She had read way too many detective novels as a kid to let something like this go.

LATE. Dark, almost midnight. The first day of the festival was long over, the seats empty and the ground cleared of litter left behind.

But there was still an energy about the place, the sort of energy that made the hair on Piper's arms stand up. She guessed that might have something to do with the rumbling in the sky, signaling the approach of a thunderstorm. There was electricity in the air.

Piper needed to stop freaking herself out, but who wouldn't be freaked out while sneaking around an ancient henge in the middle of the night?

What was she doing out there? Slinking around in the dark after following Anna and Kaden from the hotel.

Since when was Anna staying in a room with this guy?

Just like before, when Piper asked, she got a brick wall thrown up in front of her. Anna wouldn't say a word, would only promise that everything would make sense eventually.

That was cute.

Still, Piper admitted to herself as she followed the two of them at a distance that she had no idea why this was so important. Why did it stick in her craw as it did? Why couldn't she let it go? She trusted Anna. Didn't she?

She had before that day. Before she'd started acting weird, like a different person. Secretive, guarded.

She could admit to herself, too, that she was afraid this had something to do with a side deal. Maybe somebody had approached her with an offer to go solo. To ditch the band and move forward on her own.

The thing was, while Anna was a loyal sort of person, she had bigger issues at stake. Like her father. She had to pay for his care, which was something that kept her up at night. Worrying about him, feeling like she was falling short as his daughter.

If somebody had approached her with promises of a contract and a signing bonus and hefty royalties, but only on the condition that she cut ties with the band, what would she do? Where would her loyalty fall?

And Piper couldn't blame her. She really couldn't. That didn't mean she would sit back and accept being lied to, however.

It was with this in mind that she ducked and dodged in the shadows, careful to make sure they didn't know they were being followed. This Kaden had to have something to do with it. Whatever it was.

They were examining the standing stones positioned around the outer edge of the amphitheater. Anna had expressed interest in them earlier, hadn't she? One of the stones had a carving that matched one of her tattoos. She saw it as a good sign, a promise that their troubles were over.

And if she had not betrayed the band, their problems were over. Angus and Scott, the pair they had spoken with after their set, were extremely interested in signing the band to their label. Not only that, but three different big shots had slipped their business cards into her hand after that.

They had the whole world at their feet and nothing but opportunity up ahead. At least, it should've felt that way.

Piper ducked behind one of the stones when Anna and her new friend stopped in front of the very stone she had just been thinking of. The one in the middle, the one directly across from the stage down below. "Are you sure you dropped it here?" Anna whispered. The light breeze carried her voice over to where Piper hid, peeking out from behind a stone.

"Aye. I believe I did. I must have, for ye held it in the hand ye extended to me, and it fell into my palm just before I came through."

Piper strained her ears, wondering if she could possibly be hearing them right. Came through? Came through what? What were they looking for? They hadn't said yet. All they did was crouch, stirring the grass with their fingers, muttering to each other.

Thunder rumbled overhead, louder than before. Kaden looked up at the sky, and Piper ducked fully behind the stone before he caught sight of her. "Tis brewing up," he observed in that strange, affected brogue of his.

"We can't just leave it here," Anna insisted. "What if some random person picks it up and ends up going through? What if it's a little kid? They wouldn't last a day."

Well, that settled it. Anna needed to see a doctor. She had completely gone off the deep end, making no sense at all. Maybe the strain from preparing for their gig, knowing everything that hung in the balance, had broken her a little bit.

"If we canna see it, neither will they. We can return after dawn, and perhaps we will be better suited to find it."

Piper ventured another peek from around the stone and found Kaden standing with his hands on Anna's shoulders. Their bodies were practically touching, and Anna looked up at him with something much deeper than a casual acquaintance. She was in love with this guy.

She was starting to regret placing her faith in Anna, not to mention the future of their band. The girl seemed to lead a double life.

Just as she started to wonder how she would break the news to Jimmy and Ed, up ahead, Kaden turned away from the stone and started walking toward her.

She ducked around, pressing herself against the other side of the stone, holding her breath and praying they didn't hear her or see her. As they passed behind her, moving from right to left, she moved from left to right until she rounded the stone and stood behind them.

They were completely wrapped up in each other, unaware of anyone but themselves. Piper breathed a soft sigh of relief.

Just what were they looking for, though? She couldn't help herself. She had to do a little digging of her own.

As she reached the center stone, the first fat raindrops started to fall. She instantly regretted not bringing an umbrella, though she guessed she would've stood out carrying one over her head. In spite of the rain and the thunder, she dropped into a crouch and ran her hand over the grass.

What could he possibly have dropped that would have led them to come out so late at night? What was that valuable? And small enough that it wouldn't be easily visible?

If she didn't stop asking all these questions, she would go off the deep end the way Anna had. But she wouldn't be able to catch a wink of sleep if she didn't know.

2

———

Aidan McGregor had never known such misery.

It was not bad enough, he supposed, that his cousin went missing.

Nor was it bad enough, he supposed, that it appeared as though that cousin had murdered their chieftain.

No. He now had to wait in the place where Kaden had last been seen, in case his cousin decided to return.

He had not been present during Kaden's disappearance, and as such could not make sense of what he'd been told. All who had been present swore, eyes wide and voices trembling, that the man appeared to have stepped through the henge. Through solid stone. And he had not emerged on the other side.

He had simply disappeared. He no longer existed.

Aidan shook his head, laughing at this. It was not a light, humorous laugh, however. There was a great deal of bitterness behind it.

Who would not be bitter when forced to stand in a rain-storm, guarding the stone? As if it were possible for men to simply step through solid rock. He was certain the men who had claimed to witness this were half out of their minds with drink. That was the only explanation.

He pulled the hood of his cloak lower over his forehead, raindrops dripping from the fabric and landing upon his chest. In such a downpour, even the thickest cloak proved useless. He would have done better had he not worn it at all, for the sopping wool weighed heavily on him.

Though not as heavily as the weight of his thoughts.

Alone, in the middle of a raging storm, Aidan could allow himself to think that which he did not dare speak aloud.

If his cousin were still alive, and if he were to step through that very stone against which Aidan leaned at that moment, he would not report him to the rest of the clan. Instead, he would help Kaden in any way he could, that he might escape justice.

For it would not be justice. Kirk McGregor had killed Kaden's mother before his very eyes, then held him in a cell under charges of treason.

Treason! When the man had practically single-handedly seen to Clan McGregor's victory over Clan Fraser! Was that treason?

It had been years since Aidan trusted or looked up to the clan chieftain—likely thanks to the nearly constant arguing between Kirk and his father. Worse than a pair of crones, the two of them were, ever snapping at each other.

If this were only because of the differences in their temperaments, Aidan would never take offense or even given it second thought. But it was Kirk's very deliberate, very pointed taunting of the great Clyde McGregor which Aidan could not find it in himself to abide.

No matter how his father begged him against it, telling him it was for his own good, Aidan had begun to hate Kirk over the years. Once he had become a man and had begun to understand the way men such as himself thought and behaved, he could not bring himself to respect the man. It mattered not that he had been clan chieftain and as such worthy of loyalty.

In Aidan's mind, a man earned loyalty. It was not to be given to him simply because he had been born first of the clan's last chieftain.

No, if he ever saw Kaden again, he would certainly not speak of it. It was for only this reason that he had not grumbled in the least when asked to stand watch, even as black clouds piled in from the west and the air took on a strange, tight feeling which warned of flashes in the sky.

Though now, soaking wet and alone beside the henge, he could think of more pleasant ways to pass the time.

Who would be chieftain of the clan now? Kirk had no sons—no children at all, at least none who had lived. Both of his wives had died bearing him children who had also died. He had never married again, though he must've known the responsibility he held.

Like as not, there would be a great amount of argument among the men as the matter was settled. Aidan cared little for such matters and would certainly not offer his leadership in place of that which had been lost. He was no leader, and he knew it.

Kaden was a leader. Kaden was the man who had seen to the victory over Clan Fraser—no matter how many spoke in hushed whispers of the witch who had supposedly been the reason for their success.

Anna. She had disappeared as well, and from what he'd heard it had been with Kaden.

The men all believed her to be a witch, as Kirk had. What did Aidan believe? He was uncertain on that. While he knew for certain that witches existed, and had known since he was a bairn that Kaden's mother was one of them, he could not imagine one allowing herself to be held captive as long as Anna had.

In his eye, it stood to reason that a powerful person would use their powers if they had them. And that they would not waste them on such matters as seeing to one clan's victory over another.

Just the memory of that battle caused him to shiver in a manner even the rain could not make him do. He had come near to losing his life that day. Very near, indeed. Were it not for him raising his scarred wooden shield at the last moment, he might have lost an arm to the sword coming down on him. Or worse.

That had been Kirk's way. Perhaps at one time, he'd cared more for the clan than for anything else. Perhaps he had taken quite seriously his responsibility toward the men and women in his care.

Somewhere, over time, his thoughts had shifted. He began to care more for the amount of land under the clan's ownership. For the amount of wealth they could gather. For their position in the Highlands, their greatness when compared to Clan Fraser or any of the other larger, more powerful plans.

He had gone from wishing to protect his people to

wishing to grow his stature. That was when he had begun to make such foolhardy decisions as to keep a witch locked away that he might use her for the betterment of the clan—and himself.

Aidan's father would never have done that. Clyde MacGregor was a man of wisdom, using sense and logic to work his way through a problem. No man could ever call him weak or cowardly, as he had availed himself on the field of battle, just as always. Yet he knew that battle ought only to come as a result of every other effort being exhausted.

He would not have leaped into battle with the Frasers or with any clan. It was only through Kaden's cleverness and determination that they had come out victorious. Had it not been for him, and for what Aidan suspected was an affection for the lass on whom Kirk had pinned his hopes, they might easily have lost half their men that day.

For while fatigue had clearly plagued the Fraser men, they were fierce warriors who had not come by their reputation for brutality for no reason.

Yet even after all of this, Kaden had been accused of treason. Any thinking man would see through this in a moment, but men with a fierce devotion to Kirk MacGregor were not known for their love of thinking. They were the sort who would rather act first, then think later. If ever.

And they wanted blood in repayment. How quickly opinions changed. The man who had been exalted by all who knew him earlier that very day was now being hunted.

Aidan hoped he had gotten far away, that he would never come back even if it meant losing the closest thing he'd ever had to a brother.

Lightning flashed overhead, great, thick bolts that reminded him of long fingers stretching across the clouds. Again and again, lighting up the sky as if it were midday instead of nearly midnight.

He shivered again, drawing his cloak more tightly closed. He'd once seen a man struck by one of those bolts while riding across an open field.

And he had seen what had become of the man and of the horse on which he'd ridden. He had no great desire to suffer the same fate.

He would be relieved soon by another member of the clan, no doubt. And while the notion of being warm and dry appealed greatly, he dreaded the notion of his cousin being found by someone other than himself. Perhaps he could continue searching on his own. Far better for him to find Kaden and Anna, than any of the others.

He stomped his feet, doing what he could to ward off stiffness brought about by standing for so long in the rain, and looked down with a frown as his foot slid on a small stone which had nearly torn through the sole of his boot.

A jagged bolt of light flashed across the sky then, allowing him a glimpse of the carving in the stone.

A rune. This was a rune, dropped here beside the henge.

He bent to pick it up, turning the stone about in his hand. Its carving was familiar to him. Fehu.

He nearly dropped it in surprise when he realized, looking up at the stone beside which he stood, that the same symbol had been carved into the tall, thick slab.

A shiver ran up his spine, enough to make his teeth chatter. Was there something to this? What were the chances of this rune lying beside the corresponding stone merely out of accident or chance? Truly, such coincidences rarely occurred.

Yet if it were not a coincidence, what could it mean?

Perhaps either Kaden or Anna been in possession of this rune before they had—what? Disappeared? He still could not believe it, as such things simply were not possible, but the rune in his hand had made him begin to question what he believed.

He leaned one palm against the standing stone, rubbing mud from the rune with the thumb of his other hand.

And he nearly jumped from his skin when the rune began to glow as if it were lit from the inside.

Instinct told him to drop the thing, to drop it and kick it away into the darkness. To pretend he'd never seen or touched it.

Why did he not, then? Because at the moment, he could not have dropped the rune for anything in the world. It may as well have been part of his hand.

Was it lightning filling the sky then? Making everything around him glow with a strange, greenish light? He did not know. He could not keep himself from staring down at the rune as it glowed in his palm. The light brightened and brightened until it was nearly blinding.

And he blinked. And it was gone.

The rain continued to fall, the lightning to stretch across the sky while thunder rumbled the very ground beneath his feet. By now, the rune had ceased glowing. It was now only a stone in his palm.

Only the scream of a woman broke whatever it was that

held him in place. He blinked hard, shaking his head as if to clear away the remnants of a dream.

He realized then that he felt very ill, and he sank back against the standing stone when his legs failed to support him. So many things were happening all at once, he could scarcely understand it.

And still, the woman screamed. He searched the darkness until he found her standing at the next stone, both hands covering her mouth. She was soaked to the skin, as he was, and there was a look of undeniable horror in her eyes as she stared at him.

It was then that he noticed many other things, seemingly all at once. Light in the distance, for one, and a smell in the air like he had never known before. As if something were burning—a great many somethings, in fact.

It was only when he turned his head to the side to look down upon the field where he had only days before fought on the side of Clan MacGregor that he realized something was very wrong, indeed. For what had only moments earlier been nothing more than an empty field was now a great mass of chairs and benches, and a platform raised above the ground at the far end.

It had not been there only moments earlier. None of it had been, just as the twinkling lights in the distance, like hundreds of candles burning all at once, had not been there. Where had the woods gone?

"Who are you? Where did you come from?" the woman demanded, still keeping her distance.

Strange, that. For he had been about to ask her the very same thing.

3

She had to be going crazy.

He wasn't there before. She knew he wasn't there before! She had been alone, completely alone, and just about to call it a night and walk in rain-soaked shoes back to the hotel blocks from the amphitheater. She had been cursing herself, too, angry at letting herself be led into a wild goose chase.

Lightning striking nearby had made her stop, cowering next to one of the stones in the henge and hoping the damned thing didn't attract more lightning.

The next thing she knew, there he was. Slumped against the center stone, completely out of nowhere. He couldn't have sneaked up on her in the dark, could he? Had he been there all along and she just hadn't seen him, too busy looking for whatever Anna had lost?

All she knew was, he scared the crap out of her, and she had screamed before she could stop herself.

He pulled back the hood of his cloak and stared at her, still leaning against the stone and breathing heavily like he had just run a great distance. Funny, but he reminded her of Kaden. They shared the same tall, wide build, the same brown hair, the same strong features, and deep-set eyes.

And he was dressed sort of the same way, too. His cloak covered most of his clothing, but when he tried to stand up straight and support himself on his own two feet, she caught sight of the same belted tunic and tight pants. Were they in the same group? Were they friends?

That wouldn't explain why he had appeared out of nowhere.

"Answer me!" she demanded. "Are you following me? Where did you come from? Who are you?"

The man blinked, staring at her like he'd never seen a woman before. She guessed she looked a mess. Her t-shirt was plastered to her body, just like the hair now stuck to her head. She really hadn't thought this through, but then she hadn't expected the downpour, either. And she certainly hadn't imagined practically crawling around on her hands and knees in the dead of night.

"Do you know how to talk? Can you hear me?" she pointed to her ears, wondering if he might be deaf.

"Aye. I can hear ye." A deep voice, uncertain.

"Okay. Who are you? Why are you here? Were you following me?" How stupid was she? She had come out in the middle of the night without a weapon or anything at all to protect herself with. If this monster of a man tried to attack her, she wouldn't stand a chance.

"Following ye? I dinna even know who ye are, lass."

He groaned then, staggering back against that center stone as his eyes closed. "I dinna feel well, to be honest." No, and he didn't look well, either. Lightning illuminated his face—a nice face, a handsome face if his mouth hadn't been twisted in a grimace.

"Where did you come from? Who are you with?" And why did she care? If she had half a brain, she would've used his illness to her advantage and run away before he could catch her. Whoever he was, she doubted he was there to make friends. With a build like his, he would've made a good bouncer or bodyguard.

Or hitman.

But that still didn't explain what he was doing there in the middle of the night. Even as instinct screamed at her to run, curiosity held her in place. Maybe he would hold some kind of clue as to who Kaden was since all she could do when she heard this man speak was think of the way Kaden had spoken earlier. Just one more coincidence that couldn't really be a coincidence.

"I could not say," he muttered, his voice barely audible over the rain and thunder. Was he really weak and sick, or was he only pretending to be to throw her off?

"How did you get here?" she asked, looking around. He might've walked, as she did. But unless he was skilled at becoming invisible, there was still no explanation for how he had suddenly appeared in that very spot when he had not been there less than a second earlier.

He opened his mouth like he was about to give her an answer, but instead of speaking, he bent at the waist and threw up. She winced, taking a step back, looking away until the sound of his gagging died off.

Either he was really, really good at diversion—like to the point of making himself throw up on demand—or he was seriously sick and in need of help. Was that her problem, though? It wasn't like she'd asked him to appear out of nowhere and scare her half to death.

When he stopped retching she turned back to him and found that things could, in fact, be worse. Now, he was unconscious. Or pretending to be.

"You've gotta be kidding!" she called out over the rain and thunder. "Come on!"

He didn't budge. Not even when she took a few tentative steps closer and nudged his thick leg with her foot. "Hey. Hey, you. Wake up. Come on, wake up. You'll catch your death out here." She was starting to sound like her grandmother, but that didn't make it any less true. It couldn't be good for somebody already clearly sick to lie around in the rain, in sopping clothes.

He was way too big for her to move on her own. Even if she could move him, what was she supposed to do? Drag him through the street? Sure, that wouldn't attract any unwanted attention. Spending the night in jail was hardly the way she wanted to cap off this trip to Scotland.

He was out cold. Not even the smack of raindrops on his face made him stir. Something had happened to him. Maybe he had dragged himself there after an accident somewhere. Or maybe he was struck by that lightning bolt that had practically blinded her right before he appeared.

If that was the case, he needed to get to the hospital. Of course, like an idiot, she'd left her phone in her room. It would've been soaked by now, anyway, probably ruined. That wouldn't have been any more help than it was when she didn't have it on her.

Could she leave him alone while she went for help?

Should she leave him alone at all?

"Sorry, buddy," she muttered, opening his cloak and looking at him as closely as she could in darkness punctuated only by the occasional flash of lightning. He didn't look burned or wounded, and there was no blood anywhere that she could see. Just a lot of muscle which even now, soaking wet and wondering how she managed to get herself into situations like this, burned itself into her awareness.

"Do you have a wallet or phone or anything?" She patted his hips and just about jumped when she touched metal running down his leg. She pulled her hand back quickly, looking at it, expecting to see blood.

He was wearing a sword, for God's sake. An actual, honest-to-God sword. Who did he think he was? What did he think he was doing?

He was in no position to answer any questions, unflinching as the rain pelted his face. Once again, she wondered how she managed to get into situations like this.

She had one of two options. Either go on her merry way and pretend she'd never met this guy, or wake him up and figure out what to do with him afterward. That led itself to other decisions. If and when he woke up, what would she do with him? Take him to the hospital? Take him to the police, even?

He didn't look like such a bad guy, but it was easy to make that sort of judgment about a person when they were unconscious and totally helpless. Yes, she could have done just about anything to him, and he would never have known.

What if somebody came along and stole from him?

What if they took his sword and used it on him? Or on some other sucker?

Granted, she would never know, but she would always ask herself what happened to him. And whether she could've helped if he was really in bad shape.

"All right, buddy. Come on. Wake up for real now." She patted his cheeks as hard as she dared. Nothing. So she went a little harder. Harder still. Finally, when she was practically slapping him, he woke up.

And his hand shot out and grabbed her wrist, encircling it with thick, strong fingers that for a split second she thought would tighten and twist and hurt her.

They didn't. But he did hold her securely. "What are ye on about?" he grumbled. "Striking a man that way."

"You were unconscious," she reminded him. "Should I have left you out here in the rain, all alone? I could have, you know. I wish I had."

He scowled. "Who are ye?"

"I was asking you the same question. You're the one who showed up out of nowhere, not me."

"Tis yourself who is here now, where I was standing guard."

"Standing guard?" she asked. "You weren't. I've been here for ages, and I didn't see you until the lightning strike." This was officially more trouble than it was worth. She should've left him and gone on her way. She might be halfway to her room by now, where dry clothes and a warm bed waited.

"I dinna ken any of this," he muttered, finally letting her go in favor of standing. "I dinna know where I am. I dinna know this place."

He looked up at the stone, though, then to the stones standing on both sides of it. "But I know this. I know these stones. I was standing beside them before..."

"Before?"

"Before." He heaved a sigh. "Before I found ye here."

"You didn't find me," she insisted. "I found you. I was standing here the whole time, and you showed up out of nowhere."

He rubbed the sides of his face, groaning. "I canna make sense of it. I can scarcely hold a thought in my head. I need... to get out of the rain, for one," he noted, "and I need to think."

"I'm going to my hotel," she decided out loud. "I'll see you never. I'd say it was nice to meet you, but, well..."

She turned away, determined to leave him there.

But darned if she couldn't help looking over her shoulder.

And he was still standing there, looking around like he had never seen anything around him but the stone he kept touching. Like he couldn't believe it was there, in the middle of everything else. For such a big guy—wearing a sword, for that matter—he managed to look terrified. The way a little kid would look if they were suddenly out in the world without their parents.

Maybe he had been struck by lightning, after all. Or maybe he hit his head and was having a hard time remembering things.

"Darn it," she whispered, shaking her head at herself. "Come on. Can you walk? Or do you need help?"

"Nay. My legs work," he muttered, still looking around

himself like he was completely unaware of anything. "Where is this place? Where are we?"

"Edinburgh, or just outside of it. Don't you remember?" She touched his arm before wondering if that was a good move.

"Edinburgh?" he snorted. "Nay. Tis impossible."

"How?" she asked. "I mean, I know where I am. I've been here for days."

"And I have lived a short ride from here throughout my life, lass, and I can tell ye this isna Edinburgh or anything like it."

"Uh, okay." Maybe it would be better to agree with him for now, rather than arguing and wasting time. "Let's go. We have to get out of the rain, and maybe you'll feel better once you get a little rest."

"Where are we going?" he asked, though he followed close behind.

"Like I said. To my hotel."

"Hotel?"

Seriously? "Yes. Where I'm staying while I'm here. A place where people stay when they're traveling."

"Hotel," he murmured like he had never heard the word before. Maybe it was just English which challenged him?

She led the way from the amphitheater through the park which surrounded it, with her new friend muttering comments and questions to himself. He was really and truly messed up. Was it too late to find the nearest psych ward?

"What is that?" he demanded, breathless, as a truck drove past on the street beyond. Like he had never seen it before. "And what is that?" He pointed to a streetlamp.

"Okay, okay. Hang on." It might have been the middle of the night, but there was still a chance of attracting the attention of the wrong people. There were all sorts who would take advantage of a confused person. "You need to try to calm yourself down, okay?"

Now that they were around streetlights, she could see him better. And he looked flat-out horrified at every single thing around them. His eyes darted back and forth, taking in everything at once, and his chest rose and fell surprisingly fast.

"Hey. What's your name?" she thought to ask, her body tensed in case she needed to take off running. Not only did she want to know what to call him, but she hoped the question would shake him out of the panic that was seconds away from overtaking him.

"Aidan MacGregor." He stopped staring at the streetlamps and turned to her. At least he seemed a little less freaked when he was looking at her and not everything around them. "And yours, lass?"

"Piper Johnson. Aidan, I need you to try to keep it together. You don't have anything to be afraid of, okay? We'll go someplace safe where you can get some rest and maybe once you feel better, you'll be able to make sense of things. But I need you to play it cool."

"Play it cool." Like he had never heard it before and didn't know how she expected him to act.

"Just relax. Pretend you're not surprised by anything you see or hear. Okay? Can you do that for me until we're in my hotel room?"

Was she seriously considering bringing this man back

to her hotel? Her phone was there, at least, and she could call the police if she had to. Or an ambulance.

He didn't say a word, but gave her a firm nod. His jaw worked, the muscles twitching, but he looked like he would at least try to hold it together. It was better than nothing.

"Okay. Let's go." She took his hand and hoped it would look like nothing more than a couple walking back from a pub late at night. That might at least explain why Aidan was so out of it if anybody noticed them.

4

———

It was a nightmare. It simply had to be. How else could he explain what was happening?

For this world was nothing like the world he had known. Shining metal carts ran back and forth before him on hard, shining roads slick with rain. Against that shining surface shone green, red, amber lights, and the lanterns on the front of those carts which flooded his vision each time one of them passed.

They made such noise. Everything made noise. The pounding of a thousand hooves could not possibly be so loud, so startling. A great, blaring squawk nearly stopped his heart.

"It's okay," the lass murmured, squeezing his hand. "Just a car horn. Relax. You'll be okay."

Who was she? She seemed at home in this place, unaffected by its strangeness. Nothing frightened her. And here he was, a warrior, one who had cut men down with a single swing of his sword. Trembling, panicked.

If this were a dream, truly, he would have nothing to

fear. Was that not so? He need not be afraid of anything, for nothing could harm him.

Still, if this were a dream, it was the most vivid dream of any he'd ever had. His clothing was soaked through, his cloak heavy and dripping. His feet were wet, thanks to the puddles he walked through. He could smell the rain, and that burning smell which only grew stronger now that he was in the middle of this strange, frantic place. He heard the splashing and the beating of his heart, faster than he'd ever heard it beat even while mere moments from battle.

Perhaps it was not a dream, but a fever in his brain. He'd witnessed men suffering from fever, from infected wounds which left them delirious and believing themselves speaking to mothers long since dead, to sweethearts they had not seen in more than half their lives and fellow clansmen who had fallen in battle.

Was that what was happening to him, then? Had he grown ill while standing by the henge, waiting for a cousin who would likely never appear?

Would that not be just the thing? To die from illness while waiting for Kaden? When he had no intention of announcing his cousin's presence. Kaden might live and be well while Aidan died in the effort of protecting him.

No matter why he was dreaming so, he was most certainly dreaming. He had nothing to fear. Perhaps if he reminded himself of this enough times, the sights and sounds all around him would not come as such a terrible shock.

"No, we have to stop." The lass held him back when he had been about to cross one of the shining roads. "Red light. You know what a red light means, don't you?"

No. He did not. It seemed there were many rules in this dream of his. He held his tongue rather than asking for a reason why a glowing red light meant they had to cease walking.

A group of lads walked past, all of them wearing the same brightly colored tunics, and all of them seemed to have been in their cups before venturing into the out of doors judging by their swaying and loud voices. One of them cast an eye upon Piper, whose hand he still held.

There may have been a great many things he did not understand about this place, but he knew what that look meant well enough. And while the lass's garments were rain-soaked and revealed more of her body than a decent lass revealed in front of others, her hand was in his. Did that mean nothing?

She appeared to ignore the lad's leering stare, though the firm set of her jaw and the fact that her gaze remained lowered told him a great deal.

"Leave her be," Aidan growled, sizing the lad up.

"Shh," Piper begged, squeezing his hand. "Come on."

"Listen to yer woman," one of the lads jeered while the others laughed. The sword in Aidan's belt rested against his thigh, all but announcing its presence and the promise of quick retribution.

"Come on!" Piper whispered, pulling him across the road now. It seemed a glowing green light meant they could walk. What a strange place this was.

At least the lads had moved along and left her alone. "I would have cut out his jeering tongue," he growled, recalling the smug expressions on all of the lads. He could not even say which one in particular whose tongue he would have removed. Perhaps all of them.

"You can't just do things like that." She looked up at him, moving hair out of her face to get a better view. She was a bonny lass in her way, though he could not imagine why her hair was the shade of red it happened to be. Surely she had not been born with hair that color. He'd never seen anything like it in his life.

"Why canna I do such things?" he ventured. What were the rules of this new world he had dreamed? One would imagine the rules to be precisely what he wanted them to be. That he might cut the tongue from a nasty piece of work such as the lad who had leered at her with no consequences.

"Because you just can't. You'll get arrested."

"Arrested?"

"Put in jail."

He scoffed. "I dinna think so. Not if I were defending ye from one such as that."

"Yeah, well, he didn't lay a hand on me. Guys are just like that, especially drunk guys." She paused before adding in a softer tone, "But thanks. I appreciate it."

The ground beneath their feet was hard as stone, running for what seemed like miles. "What happened to the grass?" he asked. "Where has it gone?"

"Uh, I don't know. Maybe you think you're someplace you're not. Don't think about it too much."

"I dinna ken any of this."

"Like I said, maybe don't think about it right now. And I definitely don't wanna talk about it," she added from the side of her mouth, as if she did not wish to be heard while they passed a trio of lasses wearing even less than the lass whose hand he held.

"Harlots?" he asked, his head turning.

"Oh, my God, shut up!" she whispered, pulling him aside and looking toward the lasses who continued to walk as if they had not heard him.

"Are they?" he asked, intrigued. "Brazen, walking about as they do."

"Please, just stop talking already." She closed her eyes, whispering to herself before opening them again. "We're maybe a block from the hotel. Could you please stay quiet until we get there? We'll go up to my room, and I'll close the door, and then you can say any crazy things you wanna say, but only when we're alone. Don't ask me why I care whether you end up getting thrown in jail," she muttered with a scowl.

She shivered a bit, wiping the rain from her face with a trembling hand. He frowned in disappointment with himself. While his cloak was hardly much use against the rain, sopping wet as it was, the lass might at least be covered and hidden from the eyes of men.

"Wear my cloak," he offered. He owed her that much, at least. She might have left him alone.

Yet the moment he untied it from about his neck, she shook her head, eyes bulging. "No, no, that's okay. Thanks anyway." Her gaze lowered, stopping on his sword.

"This? I canna reveal this?" he asked, more confused than ever. So many rules. "Why not?"

"Because it's a freaking sword. Please. Tie that." She did it for him, reaching up to knot the strings about his throat. "And keep it closed. One more block. Just walk for one more block and go through the lobby and into the elevator without saying a single word, and I think we'll be okay."

Block? Lobby? Elevator? He decided to nod and go along with this. It was better to go through this journey with one who seemed to know better than he did how to conduct himself.

Though he was uncertain just why he would dream of a place where a man could not wear his sword in the open.

He followed her instructions, keeping his mouth shut against the questions which threatened to make themselves heard. How did these carts with the glowing lanterns on the front move without horses to pull them? How did the lanterns work? How did any of the many glowing lights all around him manage to keep their glow? They were not candles, that much he knew.

Why was everything so loud? What were these structures they walked past? In the windows were any number of things. Furnishings, or what he supposed could pass for furnishings. Garments he could not have imagined a person wearing under any circumstances.

Yet he was imagining it, was he not? All of it.

"Okay. Here's the hotel." The lass nodded, looking ahead of them. A grand structure. He tipped his head back, blinking away the lessening rain. It towered above them, higher than anything he had ever seen. It inspired awe and even a bit of hesitation. Was he expected to go inside?

Yes, he was, into a brightly-lit entry hall with shining floors and light sparkling from chandeliers hanging overhead. They were like nothing he had ever seen before, with bits of what looked like diamonds hanging down and catching the glow.

His mouth fell open at the sight of it. It was so grand, grander than anything he had ever seen. "Are ye wealthy, lass?" he breathed, his voice echoing in the large space.

"Shh!" she whispered, glaring up at him as she pulled him along. "No talking!"

"But are ye?" he asked, utterly entranced by the beauty of it all. Surely, she was a woman of great wealth.

"No! For heaven's sake." She came to a stop before a pair of doors and pressed a button in the wall.

The doors slid open, and it took all the self-control he possessed to keep himself from jumping back in shock.

"Come," she whispered, tugging his hand. Stepping through those sliding doors and beckoning for him to do the same.

"What is it?" he breathed, without crossing the threshold he looked about the inside of the box into which she'd stepped.

"You can't be serious. It's an elevator. We're going up to the tenth floor. Unless you wanna walk up ten flights of stairs, here we are."

He cringed. How was he expected to do this? She had been confident about it. She had stepped straight through. If a slight lass such as herself could manage it, he could do the same.

And he did. And pressed himself to the wall as the doors shut again and the sensation of rising caught him off-guard. He closed his eyes, but the sensation would not cease.

"Are you scared? Don't tell me you've never been in an elevator before."

"Elevator?" he whispered, asking himself when this

would end. The worst dream of his life. Nothing made the slightest bit of sense, and it was all startling. He had never so wished to go home. Perhaps if he squeezed his eyes closed and concentrated, he would open them to find himself by the henge again.

It was not to be. A chime sounded, and his eyes flew open to find they'd stopped. The doors slid apart. They were now facing a long corridor utterly unlike what they had seen in the entry hall.

"Let's go. Just a little farther now." She was whispering, looking both ways before leading him from the box. "Be quiet."

He decided it would be best to follow her command, as he had not the first notion of what to think of anything he saw and now understood that this world he dreamed of was far beyond anything he could manage on his own.

Just the notion of that elevator contraption lifting them as it had...

She reached into the back of her trousers and withdrew a card of some sort, waving it before one of the doors lining both sides of the corridor. A click, and she turned the handle and pushed the door open.

He had never been so glad to reach any place in his life, though this room of hers made just as little sense as anything else about the so-called hotel.

So many new words. Had he dreamed them all in his head?

She touched a switch on the wall, flipping it from down to up, and the room lit up as if by magic. "Are ye a witch, then?" he asked, standing with his back to the wall.

She looked at him as if he had lost leave of his senses. Which, in honesty, he felt as though he had done.

"No," she muttered, eyes narrowing. "Why would you ask me that?"

"Ye made the light go on all about the room." There was a lantern on a table, and two mounted on the wall over a pair of beds. The finest beds he had ever seen, for certain, topped with plump pillows and covered in what looked like silk.

"Which is it? Do you think I'm wealthy, or do you think I'm a witch? Let me clear up the confusion here and now by telling you I'm neither of those things. I'm just me. Plain old me."

"How were ye able to do that, then?" he demanded, asking himself as he spoke whether it was entirely wise to demand anything of a witch.

"Able to do what? Flip a light switch?" As if to prove a point, she reached over and flipped it up and down, causing the light to go on and off with each motion.

He had to sit down. His legs would no longer support him. "I dinna ken any of this," he muttered, holding his head in his hands. "I dinna know where I am or why I have come here."

"Are you trying to tell me you're from a place where this isn't normal? Electricity, cars, pavement, elevators? It's all new to you?"

"Aye," he groaned without looking up.

"So where you're from, it isn't twenty nineteen?"

"What is twenty nineteen?" he asked.

"The year, Aidan. Twenty nineteen. Two thousand and nineteen."

He had to be mishearing her. There was certainly no chance that she'd told him the year was two thousand and nineteen.

Yet when he lifted his head, looking to her, she wore an expression of utter certainty. Eyes hard and probing, arms crossed beneath a bosom all but revealed by the wet tunic she wore. She was not speaking in jest.

Which was why it took a moment for him to find his voice. "Lass, where I come from, it is sixteen hundred and sixty-five."

5

———

Piper sat at the foot of one of the double beds.

Aidan sat at the other.

Neither of them spoke a word. The silence in the room was practically deafening.

Who did he think he was trying to fool with that sixteen hundreds nonsense? It wasn't possible. He was out of his mind.

She had to call a hospital and have him picked up. It would be the kindest thing possible under the circumstances. He would only end up hurting himself out in the world, poor guy. He didn't seem to mean any harm. He was confused.

It struck her as funny that she never considered he might be lying, making all of this up to…

To what? That was why she had never considered it, because what did he have to gain by this? Would he try to attack her, now that he was in her room? He wouldn't have to go pretend to be from four hundred years in the past to do that. He was big and strong enough that he might've overtaken her at the henge or in the park.

Or right there in the room, for that matter.

But he hadn't done anything like that. In fact, he had been maybe a few seconds away from starting a fight with those drunk idiots in the street. He would've protected her with that danged sword of his.

That didn't mean he was legit. It only meant he was sincere—which meant he was sick.

She cleared her throat, which sounded painfully loud in that otherwise silent room. "Uh, maybe you should go to the hospital. Do you want me to call an ambulance for you? Or we could get a cab and go to the nearest hospital on our own."

He sighed, staring at the floor the way he'd been for ages. "I dinna ken half of what ye said, lass."

"What don't you... ken?"

"Hospital. Call. Ambulance. Cab. I dinna know what any of it means."

"Seriously?" He only lifted his thick shoulders, then dropped them again. "Fantastic. Do you trust me? Because I wouldn't do anything to hurt you. I mean that. I wanna help. Nothing I just said is anything bad or dangerous. Hospitals are where people go when they're sick. Call means using a phone, and sure, okay, you don't know what that means," she concluded.

"I dinna."

"An ambulance takes you to the hospital, and a cab. Remember the cars we saw outside? It's like that. It can take you places much faster than walking." Was this really happening? Was she explaining everyday life to this man as if his delusions were real?

It was kind, if anything. He needed a little kindness. The guy was scared to death, it was obvious, even if he tried hard not to show it.

Maybe even though he was sick, he had his pride to consider.

"I only want to help you," she whispered. "I wouldn't say any of this if I thought it would hurt. But you seemed so... out of place out there, on the street. I can't imagine you trying to make your way around on your own. The doctors at the hospital might be able to help you make sense of this."

"Ye said this hospital place is for people who are ill?" he asked, turning his head slightly that he could look at her with one eye. "Is that right?"

"Yes."

"I am not ill that I know of," he murmured. "I might be ill in my life. My real life. I thought this was a dream. All of it. How can it not be?"

Yeah, he was totally out of it. A million miles away. "I can call the front desk and have them flag a cab for us right now if you want, and we can go. I'll go with you. I won't make you do it alone." What she really wanted to do was call Anna and ask for help, but where would she begin? It would mean admitting she'd followed her and Kaden earlier, and something told her that wouldn't go over well.

"I dinna wish to go to a hospital." He said the word slowly, like he was trying to commit it to memory. Whatever was wrong with him had definitely wiped out some vital part of his brain. It was a shame, since he seemed nice enough and was handsome and healthy looking. Like he might have lived a pretty good life until he got sick in his head.

"Yeah, but I can't imagine you doing anything else. I can't take care of you."

"What is that?" He pointed to the TV. "I have been wondering about it since I sat down."

"A TV." She picked up the remote on the nightstand. "You can watch shows. Right," she muttered when he turned to her, blank-faced. Of course, he didn't have the first idea.

She turned it on, and his eyes went wide enough that she thought they might fall out of his head. His mouth went round in wonder, his breath coming in sharp little gasps as he watched the news.

And she watched him. It was like seeing a little kid discovering something for the first time. That look of complete wonder. When she flipped the channel just to see how he would react, his stunned gasp would've made her laugh if it wasn't so unsettling.

"Where did they go?" he asked, pointing to the screen. "The lass and lad who were speaking. Where are they?"

"They aren't inside the TV." She got up and went to it, waving a hand behind it. "See? It's complicated, but the people aren't inside. I promise. Everybody who turns on that channel can see them right now, but we went to a different one where different things are on."

And those different things just happened to be a pretty hot and steamy scene in a movie. She fumbled with the buttons before turning the TV off, cheeks burning, waiting for more pointed questions.

There were none. He seemed to at least understand what that was.

She stammered, blushing furiously. "So. That's TV. You're seriously telling me you've never seen one before?"

"Lass, how many times do I have to tell ye? I am not from this time. I canna ken how I could dream all of this. How could I imagine it? How could anyone?"

She sat on the bed again, facing him. "You're convinced that you came from sixteen sixty-five."

"I am certain of it, lass." He faced her, their knees almost touching thanks to his very long legs. The scene she had just accidentally stumbled upon flashed through her mind and she pushed it away. Like she needed to be thinking about that sort of stuff when this guy was off his rocker.

"What happened before you got here? What went on in your time?"

He took the question seriously, his forehead creasing as he concentrated. "Well, now. Let me think. I was standing at the henge. There was a rainstorm, as here. Lightning in the sky. I found a rune on the ground and picked it up to study it. I touched the Fehu stone—the carving in the rune was also of Fehu."

"The center stone?" she asked. He nodded. The one Anna had been so interested in.

"And then, I canna say." He spread his hands in a gesture of hopelessness. "It seemed to glow from within, as these lanterns do." He pointed to the lamp.

"It's called a lamp."

He shrugged. "As ye say. The light grew quite bright, and then I was with ye. Ye were screaming."

"Because you showed up out of nowhere."

"As ye say." There was a defeated note in his voice. "I dinna ken what is happening."

"You've said that, and I don't understand any more than you do. You're sure you were in your time? The sixteen hundreds?"

"Aye." Now, there was an edge of anger.

He suddenly stood, moving quickly enough to startle her. She leaned away from him, ready to jump up if she needed to. A lamp to the side of the head might be just what this guy needed.

He didn't make a move to hurt her. Instead, he finally took off his cloak and let it fall to the floor in a wet heap.

All she could look at was the sword hanging from his waist. An honest-to-God, freaking sword. It was longer than her arm from hilt to tip, and it looked heavy.

"What's in that?" she asked, pointing to a pouch hanging from the other side of his belt. He untied it and tossed it onto the bed.

"Here. Examine it for yourself."

She did, opening the drawstring at the top with gentle fingers. What was she going to find in there? She kept looking up at him, unsure of herself.

Inside was nothing sinister. Nothing more than a few coins which looked like nothing she had ever seen before. They were ancient by the looks of them, sort of misshapen. But shiny enough. Like artifacts, if somebody had taken the time to clean them up.

"This is all you have on you?" she asked, handing it back. "No wallet? No ID?"

"I dinna—"

"Ken what I'm talking about. Right." She clasped her hands between her knees, realizing her palms were clammy now. Was that because this Aidan person unnerved her more with every passing moment?

Or because for some completely unthinkable reason, she was starting to believe him?

It was total insanity from start to finish, but what other explanation was there? Maybe he had been struck by lightning, and it had totally scrambled his brain. That wouldn't explain him carrying nothing but a few old coins.

He wasn't injured, either, the way she would imagine a person would be after a lightning strike. Granted, she had never known anybody who got struck, but wouldn't he at least be burned a little? There wasn't so much as a scorch mark on his shirt. He looked dirty, down to his grungy fingernails.

But that was it.

"Aidan, I don't understand this," she admitted with a sigh. "I want to believe you're from this time and you're just ill, like you hurt your head or something, but that doesn't explain why you're dressed like you are and carrying that pouch and that sword. But you have to understand how unbelievable what you're describing sounds to me."

He sat again, this time leaving the sword on the floor. It landed with a solid thud. "What are ye trying to say, lass? That this is not a dream?"

"I'm trying to say this isn't a dream you're having. I don't think I'm dreaming, either. This really is twenty nineteen and..." She pinched herself. "I'm not dreaming."

He frowned deeply, his brows lowered until she almost

couldn't see his eyes, then pinched the back of his hand as she had. "I am not dreaming, either," he breathed.

"Well, crap." She stared at him. He stared at her. "What are we supposed to do now? I mean, unless we're both completely delusional, how are we supposed to move forward from this? What am I going to do with you?"

idan pressed the button on the wand—no, the remote. She had called it a remote.

He pressed it again.

Again.

It seemed there was no end to what he could find on this magic box. This TV. No matter how many times the lass had tried to explain it to him, he could make no sense of it. Invisible waves in the air, sending signals to the box and making images appear. Images of people, and the sounds coming from their mouths.

And so much! So many people, all of them appearing different from each other. Men and women wearing outlandish garments, their hair dressed in strange ways, riding in those horseless carts as if it were nothing. As if it were all normal.

He was beginning to understand that to them, it was normal.

"There is a whole world out there that you don't know about," she had told him, and never had truer words been spoken. A world in which people moved from place to place without thinking, their journeys taking nearly no time at all. She'd already told him that in this world, this future place, there were metal birds which flew through the air and carried people great distances in mere hours. Hours!

Though she could not begin to explain how the metal birds remained in the air. Not that he would have understood had she explained, for there was already so much to take in that he could scarcely imagine laboring to understand more.

All he knew was, he had sat before this box for hours while she slept, the light from it casting an eerie glow over the room.

She had tried valiantly to remain awake with him, to answer his many questions. It seemed one question always led to two more, then to two more after that as each explanation opened new possibilities. She was patient enough and had seemed willing to continue providing explanations, but there was only so much a person could do in the middle of the night.

He looked away from the TV box and over to her bed. She had fallen asleep on top of the blankets, curled up on her side and facing him. One fist was tucked beneath her chin, the other beneath the pillow.

She was a decent sort. Patient as she could be under the circumstances, he supposed. She might have left him in the rain and gone on with her life, but she had not. There was certainly no reward in this for her, yet she'd stayed up with him until her body could not manage it any longer.

He stood, pulling the top blanket from his bed in favor

of draping it over her. She sighed in her sleep, murmuring something unintelligible. Perhaps she asked herself even while dreaming just what was to be done with him.

Perhaps she might find the answer, for he was entirely unsure.

This was not his home. This was not his world. Never would he be able to manage it. How could anyone? It frightened him so. And him a grown man who had learned to fight nearly as soon as he learned to walk.

He simply had to get home. Whatever had happened to him was surely something that could be put to rights, could it not? It had to be. He could not remain here. He had a life elsewhere, and people who would look for him.

Look for him.

He sank to the bed again, holding his head in his hands. "Och, nay, nay," he whispered, careful not to wake Piper.

What if this was what had happened to Kaden? What if he were lost somewhere in this time or some other time? He had disappeared through the henge, had he not? Through the very stone against which Aidan himself had been standing just before he found himself in this strange world.

Perhaps the men who had sworn it happened were not mistaken, after all. Perhaps it had all taken place just as they had described.

It had taken place twice. And to think, he had considered them all daft. In their cups. Certainly mistaken about what they thought they'd seen.

He sat like that for a long time while the people inside the TV spoke of things which meant nothing to him. They may as well have been using an entirely different language. He would have silenced them if it were not for the strange comfort their voices provided, nonetheless. It was better than hearing nothing but the beating of his heart and the soft breathing of the lass sleeping before him.

Little wonder there was a hardness to her. She was soft beneath it, certainly, possessed of kindness. But over top of it was an edge as sharp as any blade. He thought he liked that a bit. Though it was easier to like when she was sleeping, silent, which meant she was not turning that sharpness on him.

She was not of this place. That much he knew. She had spoken of coming to this country or staying in this country as a traveler—he could not quite recall her words, as she had spoken when he was in the grip of panic. Her speech was unlike that which he heard on the TV. So she was a foreigner. She would not remain here for always.

What would he do when she left? Surely, he would not find one as sympathetic as herself. Perhaps he might find his way home before she returned to hers.

He jumped to his feet when a buzzing filled the air as if a next of wasps had been overturned of a sudden. His head snapped this way and that, looking for the source of the sound.

Piper's hand crept along the table beside the bed until it closed over the source, a slim block which she picked up and held to her ear. "Yeah?" she muttered, eyes still closed.

Until they were not closed. Until she sat bolt upright. "Oh, crap. Yeah. Okay."

She flew out of bed then, hurrying around the room, opening a chest of drawers and pulling garments from it seemingly at random. He had not sat yet, too interested in what she was doing.

"I have a meeting. I forgot about it. Damn it." She slid past him and into a small chamber which he had already marveled at. The notion of running water whenever one wanted it...

"A meeting?" he asked, standing near the door. Water ran in there while Piper muttered obscene things at herself and thumped about quite a lot.

"Yeah," she replied in a distracted manner. "It's—"

"I know what a meeting is," he grumbled. "Where? With whom?" For how long would she be away from him? What was he to do while she was gone? He could not bring himself to give voice to these questions, but they weighed heavily on him.

"The reason I'm here in the first place." She opened the door, now wearing different garments, her face freshly painted around the eyes and lips, her hair in a great mass on the top of her head. The trousers she wore left nothing to the imagination. It nearly pained him to pull his gaze from her, but there were more important matters.

"Where will ye be? Where? What am I to do while ye are gone?"

She held her hands to her head, turning in a full circle, locating the buzzing device which she had spoken into earlier and tossing it into a bag. "Just stay here. Okay? Stay. Here. Do not step foot from this room. Take a shower or something. We'll eat when I get back. I won't be long, I promise."

"A shower?"

"Jesus. Come here." She pushed past him, returning to

that small room with its running water and leaned over a tub against the wall. She turned the knobs coming from the wall. "Hot water. Cold water. Water comes out of here when you pull this knob up. Get in, undressed, close the curtain and use the soap to wash up. You could use it. Maybe I'll find new clothes for you or something since what you're wearing is a mess."

"Is it?" He looked down at himself, never having given a moment's thought to his garments.

"Just promise me you won't try to go outside. Okay? Watch TV once you're washed up. I swear I'll come back soon."

She looked up at him, and he realized for the first time that she was shaking.

He took the chance of placing his hands on her shoulders. "Are ye frightened, lass?"

"Scared to death of what'll happen if this meeting doesn't go well," she confessed. "And of what'll happen to you, which is stupid because you're not my responsibility but I hate to think of something bad happening."

"Nothing will happen." Who was he to comfort her? It ought to have been the other way around. "I will remain here. Nothing could convince me to leave, I promise ye that."

She laughed through the tears which swam in her eyes. "Okay. You're right. Wish me luck."

He had not the first notion of what she needed luck for, knowing nothing about her whatsoever. Yet he was in no place to refuse. "Good luck, lass. Be safe out there."

She laughed again, not unkindly, before leaving the room entirely.

He was alone.

He turned to gaze upon himself in the looking glass over the basin. He'd never seen himself so clearly before, and with those glowing lights all around him.

When he compared himself in his mind to the lads he'd seen on the road the night before, he could understand why Piper had advised him to clean himself. He looked as any man looked in the village, on the Highlands, every day of his life. Yet he looked nothing like those young men had.

He did not belong in this place. So many things had changed.

He peeled off his garments and worked the knobs on the wall, over the tub, before finding what he supposed was the correct warmth. Water simply flowed, so simply and easily. Little wonder washing was so ordinary among these people when it was so easily done.

It meant little, however, for if he could not be home among his people, no amount of warm water or TV or magic lanterns which turned on and off with the movement of a switch could make up for that loss.

7

"What's going on with you?" Anna stared at Piper, who ran across the lobby from the elevator. "You look like you saw a ghost."

She had. She had seen a man who was basically a ghost. He would've been dead for hundreds of years. Only he wasn't. He was in her room, figuring out the very tricky art of taking a shower.

A crazy, nervous giggle threatened to bubble up out of her mouth. She was going to lose her grip.

"I'm okay," she managed to choke out, clenching her fists and digging her nails into her palm to center herself. "Really. I'm good. I overslept like an idiot."

"You don't look like you slept at all." Anna led the way out of the hotel.

"Gee, thanks. You look great, too." In fact, she looked like she had also spent a sleepless night. Maybe she and Kaden had decided to do some more late-night exploring. Of course, she wasn't supposed to know about that.

"It's been a crazy few days," Anna admitted as they bundled themselves into a cab.

"I'm looking forward to getting home." Piper rested her head against the seat, eyes closing. Her head was splitting. If she had gotten more than two hours of sleep, it would be a miracle.

No matter how she tried, she couldn't get his face out of her head. His voice. His fear. He was this huge guy, like a mountain, who could probably slice somebody in two with that sword of his. But there was something about him that brought out her protective side.

It didn't make any more sense than anything else that had happened so far.

She checked the time on her phone. What was he doing? There was no way for him to reach her if he needed anything. Not like he would've known how to use a phone even if she'd had the chance to explain it to him, which she hadn't. He probably would've asked her a hundred questions about how the phone worked and where the voices came from until her eyes would cross and she would regret ever having brought it up in the first place.

"You have a date I don't know about?" Anna joked, noticing the number of times Piper looked at her phone. In less than a day, they had completely changed places. It was Anna who'd acted like she had a screw loose after their gig at the festival.

Now? Piper could only imagine what was going through her friend's head.

"Like you said, it's been a long couple of days." And they were supposed to fly home the following morning, too. She would have to leave him behind. What was he going to do?

She thought maybe calling the hospital and having him admitted was still a decent idea, since he would at least be safe there.

Based off what she had seen of him so far, he would end up getting into a fight with a guy for looking at a girl the wrong way and find himself in jail in no time. Or dead.

She considered talking to Anna about him. She needed to get some of the crazy thoughts out of her head and into somebody else's head. Maybe Anna would have an answer, or at least an opinion on what should be done with this supposed time traveler.

Time traveler. She would never have guessed such a thing was possible.

But no, because she would have to come out and admit why she had been at the amphitheater at that time of night. She didn't have it in her just then to come up with a lie, especially not with a lie that made any sense and wouldn't come off as a lie right away.

Instead, she sat there feeling like she might burst open. It was so heavy, this secret, and it swelled inside her. It weighed her down, made it hard to keep her head up.

They arrived at the restaurant where they were supposed to meet up with the executives and Piper took a few deep breaths as she climbed out of the car. She had to clear her head. She couldn't screw this up.

Aidan would be hungry. She should've ordered something for him to eat before she left. There hadn't been time.

She had to stop thinking about him or else this entire trip would be for nothing. That incredible, heady, breathless exhilaration she'd felt after their performance would all be for nothing. Silly her, thinking what really mattered was making a good impression on anybody who might be watching them at the festival.

Really, it was a matter of closing the deal.

For once, it came as a relief that Jimmy and Ed would be with them. They could do the talking, along with Anna. Nobody paid attention to the bass player, anyway. All she could do was look and sound as interested as possible while trying not to look too obvious as she checked the clock on the wall like her life depended on it.

Sadly, it wasn't her life, even if it felt like it.

"AIDAN?" She barely trusted herself to speak above a whisper as she ran into the room. "Aidan? Where are you?"

He wasn't on the bed, and the TV was off. She thought for sure he would've passed the time by watching TV. Something to make him feel less alone.

He wasn't there. He left, even though she'd forbidden him to step foot outside of the room. What did he have in mind? Was he trying to get himself killed?

When the bathroom door opened, she fell onto the bed in what might as well have been a faint. Exhaustion and relief were too potent a combination. She couldn't stand up under the weight of them.

"Lass. Are ye well?" He came to her, plodding on heavy feet before standing over the bed. Her eyes were closed, but she could feel him there. He had a strong presence, for sure.

"I'm fine. I thought you left for a second there and about a hundred terrible thoughts ran through my head all at once." She opened her eyes—then gasped at what she saw.

He was wearing nothing but a towel around his waist. His hair was clean, still damp, hanging down to his shoulders in waves of dark brown with a touch of copper. And he had shaved. She'd seen a knife in his belt and guessed he must have used it.

He never would've recognized her razor if he found it.

He was beautiful. As simple as that. Morning sunshine poured through the window and turned his tanned skin to bronze. He could've been a statue, something carved or molded and polished until he shone.

He seemed completely unaware of how beautiful he was, too. Completely without an understanding of why she stared the way she did. He blinked, his hazel eyes sparkling in the sunlight. "What is the matter with ye now?"

Oh, if he only knew. "Nothing. I, um, wasn't expecting you to be practically naked when I came back."

"Ye made it sound as though my garments were not—"

"No, you're right. You're right. And I was in such a hurry to get back to you, I forgot to look for clothes. I wasn't alone, either, so I wouldn't have had a chance if I remembered. I can go out to find you something now, if you want." Anything to get him covered up. Not that the sight of his body was exactly repulsive, but that was the problem.

She sat up with a sigh, looking around the room. "Did you get any rest at all? You couldn't have slept."

"How do ye know I did not sleep?" he asked with a faint smile.

"You covered me with your blanket—and thanks for

that—and the pillows weren't touched. They still haven't been. You must be hungry and tired."

"I am, at that. I canna bring myself to close my eyes. There are too many thoughts going on." He sat on the bed across from her.

She looked away when it was obvious that he was about to manspread in his towel. "Uh, can you... cover yourself?" she asked. Her face burned, even though he was the one who should be embarrassed.

"Och, forgive me," he grunted. "Ye might look now."

She burst out laughing to find him holding a pillow in front of his thighs. He shrugged.

"As ye said, they had not been touched."

"Yeah, I guess that's as good a use as any," she agreed, shaking her head. It was nice to laugh. A release. Otherwise, she might've burst from trying to hold it all in.

"Did all go well with your meeting?" he asked.

"Oh, yeah. I think it did." She had a hard time remembering what happened. It all went by in a blur, and she had barely been paying attention to any of it. "I think they want to sign us. To a contract. They have offices and a studio in America, where we live."

He had no idea what she was talking about, but he smiled like he at least got the feel of it. "That sounds bonny. What do ye do?"

She almost laughed again. Right. He didn't know anything about her. "I play music. In a band. The people we met with today want to pay us to do it."

"Och, that does sound bonny. Will they pay ye well?"

"I hope so, but anything would be better than what we make right now, which is practically nothing. Anna really sold us today. And yesterday, when we performed. I think she was the reason they liked us so much."

"Anna?"

"She's our singer."

"I see." He frowned a little, like the name meant something to him.

"I was worried. She was just as distracted yesterday as I was today. She couldn't get her head out of the clouds for anything. I mean..."

She stopped. Kaden. Anna had been worried over Kaden the way...

And the way he looked at her, like he was afraid to let him out of her sight.

And the clothes he was wearing, so much like what Aidan wore.

The way they spoke was the same, in that affected brogue.

And if he had come through from the past, he had come through by touching the center stone in the henge. Which was where Anna and Kaden had been looking for something.

"Hang on a second. Wait here. Don't move an inch." She ran out of the room and down the hall before Aidan had the chance to ask where she was going.

Why hadn't she thought about it before? Oh, right, because she was half out of her mind with exhaustion and worry for him. Trying to decide if he was the one with the problem or if it was her fault for believing his story.

Anna's room was on the other end of the hall, past the elevator. She banged the side of her fist against the door. "Anna? I need you. It's important."

"What's wrong?" Anna called out before opening the door. "What happened?"

"Where did Kaden come from? Is he here?" She looked over Anna's shoulder to catch sight of him standing by the window, dressed just like he had been when she saw him at the festival. The clothes! She should've at least remembered the clothes.

"What do you mean, where did he come from?" There was a lot of suspicion in Anna's voice—which if anything confirmed what Piper suspected. That suspicion came from wanting to take care of him and protect him, not to mention herself.

"Where did he come from? I wouldn't ask if there wasn't a serious reason for wanting to know." She looked at him then. "Did you come from someplace in the past?"

"Are you joking?" Anna asked.

At the same time, Kaden nodded. "Aye. I did that."

"Kaden!" Anna whispered, looking back over her shoulder.

"Why do ye believe she is asking?" he demanded. "Do ye believe she imagined this on her own? Aye, lassie. Why do ye ask? What do ye know?"

She had to hold onto the wall for support. It all made perfect sense now, as insane as it still was.

It was still hard for her to form the words that she could barely believe were about to come out of her mouth. "Because I think I have somebody in my room who comes from your time."

8

When the door opened behind him, he expected to find Piper hurrying back to him.

Instead, he found the last person he would ever have expected—and the one he wished to see more than any other. "Kaden?" he whispered, disbelieving.

"Aidan? How is it possible?" He sat on the other bed as Piper had. "What is this? How did ye manage it?"

He could not find his voice. It was all too difficult to imagine, much less to speak of. "Ye are asking the wrong man. I canna say. There is no knowing."

"I ken what ye mean."

Yet he had his cousin before him, someone he knew. Someone to hold him in place as the world spun out of control all around him. "What is this time? Where have we come to?"

"Tis Anna's time," Kaden explained. "Though I feel sorry for ye. At least she explained some of it to me before I came through with her."

"Ye came through as I did, then," he breathed.

"Indeed. I never dreamed ye would follow me."

"I did not intend to. It was an accident. I picked up the rune—"

"The rune!" Kaden slapped his forehead. "I must have dropped it, then, before I came through. Did you bring it with ye, man?"

"I dinna know. I canna recall having it with me when Piper found me."

"Aye. She followed us to the henge last night," Kaden explained. "We were searching for the rune, thinking I had dropped it there."

"Ye did at that. On the other side, in our time." He searched his cousin's familiar face for understanding, gladder than he had ever been to see him. Yet no less confused than he had been before. "How can ye make sense of it?"

"I canna. I have only been here a day. Hours longer than ye, but not so many hours."

"Of course. T'was only hours since ye vanished."

"Ye believe ye held the rune in your hand when ye came through?" Kaden asked. "We might find it there before anyone else has the chance. The park will open soon for the festival, and someone else might find it."

He understood without being told how dreadful this would be. Someone might find the rune and... what? Find themselves in the past? Or they might never use it at all but keep it for themselves, leaving Aidan in this time whether he wished to remain or not.

Or none of this might happen, for the rune might not have any power at all. How were they to know?

"We ought to return to search for it," Aidan decided. For

the first time since finding himself in this new place, he felt as though he were in control of something. He was not simply waiting for things to happen, but was instead taking action on his behalf.

"I agree with ye." Kaden looked him up and down. "But ye might wish to dress before we do."

Aidan was far too glad to be with someone he knew. He could not bring himself to scowl at his cousin. "What do ye think of this time?" he asked, also glad to have someone with him who understood what it meant to be thrust into an entirely different world.

Kaden snorted. "Tis loud."

"Aye, awfully so." Aidan fetched his garments and hurried about putting them on. He might be home soon. Where he belonged, for good and for all. "I want nothing to do with it. I would like to forget it exists."

Kaden did not share this opinion; at least, he remained silent. Aidan turned to him while in the act of putting on his tunic. "I suppose ye dinna feel the same," he observed.

"Nay. I dinna." Kaden shrugged. "What can I say? I followed Anna because I wished to do so. T'was no mistake, not as it was for yourself."

"Ye might have been killed if ye remained."

"Aye, though it was not only for that that I took Anna's hand and followed her here. I could not imagine staying anywhere she was not. It would have meant nothing to me, remaining in that time without her. No matter what came of me there—whether I was caught and blamed for Kirk's death or not—it would mean nothing without her."

"It was still quite a thing to do. Ye must have asked yourself what would become of ye." Aidan stopped for a time, concentrating on his cousin rather than continuing to prepare himself. "Did ye not?"

Kaden chuckled knowingly, a wry smile twisting his mouth. "Aye. But there was no time to concern myself with it, ye ken. I had to make a choice, and quickly, and I know it was the correct choice. I am certain of it."

"The correct choice for ye," Aidan observed as he finished dressing. "Not for myself."

"As ye say," Kaden agreed, standing. "Anna was cross with Piper for following us to the henge, and for not speaking a word of ye today. I felt sorry for the lass, to be certain. She did what she could to help ye and was scolded for it. I, for one, am glad she followed us. Ye did not need to be alone. Were it not for her ye might... I dinna wish to speak of it."

"Nor do I wish to think of it." Aidan nodded to the TV. "And what do ye think of that?"

Kaden shivered. "How do ye believe they get the people inside?"

Piper and Anna joined them. Aidan could scarcely believe his eyes. He had seen the lass while Kirk kept her locked away in the stables, her wrists in iron, and had certainly seen her before riding down the slope to meet with Clan Fraser.

While washed and in fresh clothing, she looked much better than he recalled. "Hello," he smiled. "This is a surprise."

"For both of us." She grinned. "I'm glad you're doing all right. Piper took good care of you."

"Ye ought not plague the lass for it," he warned. "She

was kinder to me that she needed to be. She might have, eh, called for an... ambulance to send me to the hospital."

Over Anna's shoulder, Piper grinned and nodded.

So he had gotten it correct.

"We'll go to the henge now," Anna decided, looking thoughtful. "We should be able to find the rune, I hope. And send you back through."

"I canna wait." Although when he looked to Piper, a twinge of guilt held him in place. She had been good to him and he had nothing to offer her in return but his thanks. It seemed she deserved something more than this.

He was about to ask Kaden to give them a moment alone when Kaden sat down again, hard enough this time to bounce on the bed. He stared at the wall in front of him, his mouth open slightly. He wore the look of a man who could not quite understand what he was thinking.

"Kaden?" Anna went to him, touching his back. "What's wrong? Are you okay? Do you need something?"

He swallowed, blinking hard. "When do ye think... That is to say, when do ye believe ye might return to? What time? When?"

Aidan looked about himself. "I could not say."

"What are you thinking?" Anna asked, crouching beside him. "What do you have in mind?"

He looked to her at last, eyes moving over her face as he tried to understand what he thought. "Mam," he breathed. "What of her?"

Aidan was beginning to understand, though he had not the slightest notion of what might occur.

Piper, however, had no understanding. "What are you saying? Who is Mam?"

"His mother," Aidan murmured, turning to her. "She was killed just before..."

She was a clever lass, for certain. She understood right off, reaching for Aidan's hand and squeezing tight. "He wants to go back and save her? Oh, my God..."

He wondered whether she knew she was holding his hand. She did not look down or even express surprise. She appeared just as stricken and confused as Kaden and Anna did, the two whispering between them.

It seemed Kaden was more excited with every moment over this notion. "She need not die. We can make certain she does not die at Kirk's hand or anyone's hand."

"If we get there before that time happens," Anna murmured in a soothing tone. "We shouldn't get our hopes up. We might not make it back before Kirk did what he did. You have to keep that in mind. And what happens if we get there and it's too late, and everybody's still after you for killing Kirk?"

He scowled, though not for the reason Aidan expected. "We? I dinna recall saying ye would join me."

"You think I would let you go alone? What happens if you can't get back?"

"Then ye would be forced to remain with me, there!"

She gripped the back of his neck with one hand, pulling him closer and touching her forehead to his. "And you came here, with me, when we didn't think there was any chance of you being able to ever leave. Do you think I wouldn't do the same thing for you now that the shoe's on the other foot? I can't stand the thought of living without you. Even if I get stuck there, I would be stuck with you. That's all that matters."

She looked to Piper. "I'm sorry. I know this puts you in a bad spot, but—"

"But nothing. I'm coming with you. This is way too interesting for me to hang back on." Piper looked up at Aidan, shrugging. "My grandmom's maidens name was MacGregor, and her family came from Scotland. Isn't that interesting? I wonder if we're all from the same family."

Aidan found it difficult to share her enthusiasm. "Lass, 'tis a different time. A different world. As different from this place as ye can imagine. There is nothing of what ye are accustomed to. None of this." He flipped the switch on the wall, making the room light up and darken at will.

She giggled. "I think I can stand it for a little while if you can stand this for a little while. I would try to come back, of course."

"There's no reason why the rune and the standing stone wouldn't work again, if it worked to let Aidan through," Anna reasoned. "It's a shame we didn't have the chance to find out more about the rune and what it does."

"Perhaps now, we can. Perhaps we can spare my mam what was done to her. We can ask anything we wish to know." Kaden's eyes glowed with a near feverish light.

Aidan knew that light well, had seen it a hundred times. Once his cousin was truly determined to do something, there was no stopping him.

He would save his mother's life or die trying.

9

<hr>

J ust when Piper thought nothing could surprise her anymore. Just when she thought she couldn't possibly do anything wilder than she already had.

Now, she was on her way back to standing stones. And she wanted to use them to go back a few hundred years into the past. No big deal.

What got her about this was how cool Anna was with the whole thing. Now that they'd had a little time alone, just the two of them, she understood why Anna had seemed so different just before they went onstage. And how she'd had the time to grow her roots out.

Was this all seriously starting to make sense? Was she really buying into this?

Evidently, because she already imagined what the sixteen hundreds would look like.

"Is it scary?" she whispered up to Aidan, who walked next to her.

Neither of the guys were okay with the idea of getting into a car. It was way beyond them, even though Piper had pointed out to Aidan that he would be the only guy in the seventeenth century who had ever ridden in one.

He hadn't seemed as impressed with the idea, looking at every car and truck that passed them on the street like it was the Grim Reaper coming to collect him.

Which was probably why he looked down at her with surprise all over his face. "Scary? Frightening, ye mean?"

"Yes."

"Nay," he laughed. "Compared to where we are now? 'Tis nothing. Scary." He laughed after repeating the word. "As if anything there could be half as frightening as what ye have here."

"Um, it's a little scary," Anna whispered over her shoulder. "Sometimes. But you won't be there alone like I was, so it should be easier for you."

"What did ye find so frightening?" Kaden asked. It was one of the first things he'd said since he had the idea about saving his mom.

"Gee. Where to start? The iron shackles, for one thing. Being accused of being a witch. That was fun. Especially knowing the sort of things that happened to witches back then." She scratched her head. "Hmm. Who was the one who told me about that?"

"Verra well," Kaden grunted. "What was I to believe, seeing ye as ye are? Women of our time dinna paint their bodies unless they are witches."

"I can't believe you had to go through that on your own," Piper mused. "That's awful. You must have been so scared."

"Yeah. Extremely. I was afraid I'd end up dead before I

could get back here. And that I would let you all down."
Kaden draped an arm over her shoulders.

"So you didn't lose even a second? Even though weeks passed on that side, not even a second passed here?"

"No. In fact, I saw myself getting electrocuted on stage and falling off it. And I vanished."

Piper thought this over as best she could. "So wait. You looped back? Like, there's a version of you going through what you went through back there right now."

"Oh. I mean, I guess?" Anna looked back at her. "I guess that's what happened? But hey, everything turned out for the best, anyway." She nuzzled up to Kaden, who smiled down at her.

Bonkers. Falling in love with somebody who lived centuries ago. Anna was a smart girl, so she must have thought of this already and asked herself all the questions. Did Kaden have a grave somewhere in Scotland?

Now that he was in the present time, would his grave suddenly be empty? Should she even be thinking about this? It was enough to give her a headache. But she couldn't help it. Anybody would wonder the same things, wouldn't they?

She couldn't stop thinking about that other version of Anna currently in the past. It made her wonder if they would run into that Anna when they went through the standing stone. Or what else might be different once they showed up there.

"Are you sure you want to do this?" Anna asked as they entered the park. Plenty of people were already lining up, with others walking down the sidewalk and strolling along the grass. Normal people, people who only cared about the festival and nothing else. They had that luxury. Their lives hadn't been turned upside down by something completely inexplicable. Something they wouldn't have believed possible just a day earlier.

Impossible or not, unbelievable or not, it was also sort of exciting. She was going to go through time. She was actually going to step back in time and see things no person from her time had seen. The sorts of things history books couldn't describe. Things a person would have to see for themselves, to touch and taste and smell for themselves.

"What do you eat there?" she asked all of a sudden. What had she thought about that before?

Anna laughed, even though the question was intended for Aidan. "Let's just say everything tastes better when you're really hungry and it's either eat or starve."

"Oh, great."

Aidan shrugged. "Ye dinna have to come."

"But I want to."

"Are ye certain of that? It will be challenging. Quite challenging, indeed. Nothing like this strange, soft world in which ye live. Walking about on roads of stone," he snorted.

Kaden snickered with a look over his shoulder. "You press a button and your waste is washed away."

Anna elbowed him. "Gross."

"Is it, then? I seem to recall ye using a bucket—"

"Don't remind me," Anna warned, and there was no humor in her voice anymore. "There are a lot of things about that experience that I would rather forget, and that's one of them."

Piper decided it would be better not to ask for any further information on that particular point. She wasn't a child. She could figure things out on her own. Of course, there was no plumbing. Everybody knew that was a filthy time. And considering how filthy Aidan had looked when he first showed up, he had only confirmed this impression.

He looked down at her again, and this time he frowned with what she guessed was concern. "Are ye utterly certain? Ye dinna seem the type to take well to such a life."

He was right. He was absolutely, one-hundred-percent right. She had never so much as spent a day camping outdoors all her life. In fact, when the other girls in school joined Girl Scouts and went on camping trips with their families and even went for walks in the woods, she always wrinkled her nose and rolled her eyes and wondered why anybody would choose to spend their time with bugs and insects and creepy crawling creatures.

There were so many more interesting, comfortable, insect-free things to do. Like reading or watching TV or playing games on the computer. Though she hadn't had the luxury of a computer until she was old enough to work and save up for it herself. And she never had the sort of parents who took their kids camping or signed them up for Girl Scouts.

Still, it annoyed her that he thought he knew her so well. He had that smug tone in his voice, too, like a grown-up talking to a little kid who thought they could fly just because they wore a blanket tied around their neck and called themselves Superman.

She heaved a heavy sigh, shaking her head. "Don't worry about me. I'll do just fine. Besides, it's not like I plan on staying there for the rest of my life. I just don't see any reason why you all should get to have all the fun, and I should have to stay behind."

Kaden chuckled. "Ye had best leave the lass alone, cousin. Ye will not win an argument with one such as herself."

"And how would you know?" Anna asked, arching an eyebrow.

He only smiled, chucking her under the chin. "How do ye think?"

Sometimes they were a little bit too cute for their own good, and she had only known they were a couple for maybe two hours. Piper wondered if thinking that way made her a disloyal friend. Shouldn't she be nothing but happy that Anna found the man she was meant to love?

She happened to glance up at Aidan, wondering what he thought. The upward quirk of his mouth combined with the gathering of his bushy eyebrows told her she wasn't the only one thinking along those lines. It made her feel a little better, knowing she wasn't alone.

They reached the standing stones. To Piper, all of them looking a little taller than they had the day before. A little bigger around. A little more ominous.

That was ridiculous. Stones were inanimate. It wasn't like they held grudges or had bad intentions. But they were definitely more important to her than they had been just hours earlier.

"I wonder if any of the others do the same thing," she mused out loud, now afraid to so much as let her fingertips brush across the surface of the stones as they walked past. For all she knew, she would end up sucked into another time with no way to get back.

"Perhaps they do. Though I suspect the rune had something to do with it," Kaden theorized as they reached the center stone.

"But Anna wasn't carrying a rune when she first went through," Piper pointed out as the four of them crouched in the grass, looking around for the stone Aidan had dropped.

"True, but I have the symbol on my arm." Anna patted her ink, her eyes focused on the ground.

Piper wondered what an outsider would think about the four of them crawling around, two of them dressed like they came out of a historical costume drama.

With any luck, they wouldn't be crawling around for long, and there wouldn't be any chance of anyone finding them.

"Found it!" Aidan held up the stone in triumph. "Had I not been so dazed after coming through, I might not have dropped it at all."

Kaden groaned as he got to his feet. "Aye, I felt the same way."

"Did you throw your guts up?" Piper asked, smirking at Aidan when she remembered him heaving all over the place. Then, she stopped smirking. "Crap. Will we get sick when we go through?"

Anna shook her head. "I didn't. But who knows?"

"Ye have nothing to fear," Kaden assured her. "We will take care of ye."

As if to prove the point, Aidan moved a little closer to her.

She didn't know how she felt about that. He seemed like a decent guy, and she saw the irony in their positions reversing once they went from her time to his time. She had been the one taking care of him when he first came through, and now he would do the same for her.

Still, she couldn't see herself stepping back and letting a random stranger think he could protect her or tell her what to do. He was from a time when men did that sort of thing, wasn't he? Probably only the fact that he had been scared out of his wits would've allowed him to rely on her at all.

Now that they were going to his time, to his world with its rules, he would probably feel a lot different about it.

Just the idea of him getting all aggressive and possessive made her grit her teeth and brought to mind the men her mother had paraded through their apartment over the years. Aidan wasn't one of them. He was nothing like them. But nobody could've blamed her for being a little hand shy when it came to men with strong personalities.

This was the choice she was making, wasn't it? She guessed she could put her irritation aside long enough to experience what she would otherwise have never gotten the chance to experience.

She looked around, worried somebody would see them. Meanwhile, Anna and Kaden talked about how they would manage to make it through.

"How did you do it? What were you doing when you came through?" she asked Aidan.

"As far as I can remember, I was touching the stone with one hand while holding the rune in the other." For all the reverence they used when they talked about the thing, Piper found it hard to believe the tiny little rock with the symbol carved into it was that powerful or important.

Anna nodded, chewing her lip in concentration. "Okay. I guess we should try that. Let's all, I don't know. Hold hands?" She took Kaden's hand in one of hers, then grabbed Piper with the other. Piper took Aidan's free hand, knowing her palm was sweaty but not caring very much just then. Whose palm wouldn't be sweaty at the thought of going someplace they had never been before? Someplace where none of the rules they had grown up with applied?

She wanted to believe Aidan, but couldn't help thinking it remained to be seen just how well things would be. Sure, it was a nice thought. Putting her trust in someone, believing in him and his ability to keep her safe on this journey.

She hoped he wouldn't take it personally if she didn't quite believe him.

He then touched the fist in which he held the rune to the center stone. A greenish light started glowing from inside the closed fist, a light which Piper couldn't take her eyes from. It was hypnotic, pulling her in even as she wanted to cry out in surprise that something was actually happening. There really was a power to the rune and the standing stone.

The light got brighter until it almost blinded her. She held onto Anna and Aidan tighter than ever and closed her eyes.

It was nothing more than a stirring of air. That was it. That was the only difference she felt. There was no shudder, no shaking of the earth or rumbling or anything like that. Just a stir of air, nothing more than the slightest breeze.

Anna shook her. "We made it."

Still, she didn't want to open her eyes. She knew it was silly, but she couldn't help it. What was she going to see?

"Lass, ye can open your eyes now. All is well." The relief in Aidan's voice reached through the haze of confusion in her head and stirred her out of it.

Still, she went slowly. And at first glance, everything was just where it should've been. The same bird sounds, the same ground under her feet.

Just as quickly, though, the differences started making themselves known. The air smelled sweeter, which she knew almost instantly was thanks to there being no cars or buses or factories. She looked out over the amphitheater to find there was no amphitheater. It was nothing more than a bowl-shaped stretch of empty land.

And in the distance, where the city had only stood moments earlier, there was nothing. Trees, sure, and rivers and lochs.

But that was all she saw.

"Home." She thought she had never heard anyone sound so relieved to say a single word in all her life. Aidan might as well have been a different person, his face shining with relief in the sense that he was where he belonged.

And for just a second, it hit her in a funny way that this was the end. Once they found Kaden's mom and made sure she knew better than to show her face around Kirk, Piper would go home, and she would have to forget about him.

Because she would know that he didn't exist. That he hadn't really existed for hundreds of years.

There she went again, overthinking.

"What do you think?" Anna asked, sounding sympathetic.

What did she think? How much time did she have?

"It's... different. Do you think we came through at the right time, though? How will we know?"

Kaden looked like he was about to say something, then the ground started shaking under their feet. Piper reached out and grabbed hold of Aidan before she could think about it, wondering why they forgot to tell her about the earthquakes that took place in their time.

It wasn't an earthquake, and before she knew what was happening Kaden was gathering her and Anna and shoving them in the direction of the nearest bushes.

"What's happening?" she asked, hearing the terror in her voice and knowing there was plenty of reason for it if Kaden looked as nervous as he did.

He turned to Aidan and held out his hand. Aidan didn't need to be told what he wanted. He tossed the rune to Kaden, who placed it in Anna's palm.

"You know what to do," Kaden said, before turning away and joining Aidan by the stones.

"What's happening?" Piper whispered to Anna as they crouched in the bushes.

Anna didn't say anything at first, only pulling the hood of Piper's sweatshirt over her hair. "They'll think we're witches," she finally hissed.

Oh. Right. Piper pulled the drawstrings tight, covering as much of her head as she could. They clasped each other's hands, neither of them breathing very much, and waited to see who was coming.

Hopefully, they were friend, and not foe, she thought as the sunlight hit Aidan's sword and made it shine.

10

Aidan wiped sweat-slick palms on his trousers, waiting for the horsemen to reach them. Their own men, no doubt.

"Pretend nothing is amiss," Kaden whispered as if it needed to be said.

Aidan wondered how it would be possible to pretend such a thing after all he had just experienced and was still experiencing. How could he return to thinking and speaking and behaving as he had before accidentally falling through time and seeing what would become of the world long after his death?

The familiar sight of his father riding at the head of the group sent tears springing to his eyes. For one moment, alone in that hotel room while Piper slept and the people inside the TV had spoken of that which he could not understand, he had thought of his father and of the fact that he would never see the man again.

With that came the question of what Clyde MacGregor would think had come of his son. The notion of never knowing, always wondering. Even now, having returned, his chest ached at the thought.

Clyde pulled up short, staring down at the pair of them. "What is this, then?" he demanded before looking over his shoulder.

"What is what, Da?" Aidan asked, doing all he could to sound carefree.

"Were ye not just behind us?"

"Behind ye?" Kaden laughed. "Nay, man. We are here before ye."

"Where are the horses, then?" he asked, scratching his head. By now, several of the others had joined him, and all of them wore the same looks of confusion.

Aidan exchanged a look with his cousin. "We rode ahead, did no one speak of it?" he asked with a shrug.

"Aye, did ye not know?" Kaden's face betrayed nothing. He was a far better liar than Aidan would have believed.

Clyde scratched his head again, looking from one of them to the other before shaking his head as if to clear the confusion. "So be it. Have ye spoken to Kirk, then?"

"To Kirk..." Aidan looked to his cousin again, and this time Kaden had no quick response in hand. He was just as puzzled. "Nay. We didna see him yet. We thought ye might wish to be there."

"Aye, so I would," his father replied. "Come. We must warn him of the approach of Clan Fraser."

So that was it. That was when they had returned. To the moment Anna first stepped foot in their time.

"Aye," Kaden agreed. "We shall follow."

The men passed then, taking no notice of the pair in

the bushes. "We canna follow," Aidan reminded Kaden once the last of the riders had gone on.

"I know it, but we canna make the journey to my mam without mounts, either," Kaden countered. "And we must at least pretend to take an interest in the concerns of the clan. Just as we normally would have. If not, we will have Kirk to answer to."

Aidan saw the sense in this. "Verra well, but is it safe to leave them here?"

"That is why I gave the rune to Anna. She can always escape with Piper if need be." He went to the bushes then, bidding the lasses stand now that the threat had passed.

He could not ignore the way Piper shivered, and he so wished he might relieve her fears. It would be nothing more than empty words. Try as he might, he could not control who happened to pass them by or what would be done should that happen.

"What are we going to do?" Anna took Kaden's hand. "This is the time when I came through, isn't it?"

"Aye, which means the men are on their way to Kirk MacGregor's home. He and Clyde will argue over the best course of action now that Clan Fraser is on the march. We shall secure mounts in the village and bring them here, as the journey to the cottage will take much longer on foot. Promise me ye will both stay where ye are and not venture from this place."

Aidan looked to Piper, whose wide eyes and half-open mouth betrayed the shock she struggled with. He wished there was time to comfort her, as he would have liked to be comforted in his first moments after going through the stone into the future.

This was mere folly, however. She was not alone. She had her friend, and she had the luxury of knowing what she would find on the other side. Her situation was nothing like his. No one had warned him of what would happen or what he would find.

Even so, he could not help wishing there was something he could say to make it easier. Or that he might stroke her cheek or offer her an embrace, as Kaden could do for Anna.

"Trust me, we're not going anywhere." Anna looked to Piper, whose head bobbed up and down in a manner which would have struck him as humorous were the situation not so dangerous. He supposed that was indeed the case, that the two of them would not dare venture from that place for fear of what might befall them.

"We shall not be long." Kaden kissed Anna briefly, fiercely, before turning away. And again, Aidan felt as though he ought to do or say something for Piper. It was not his place, he was aware of this, but the sense of falling short remained.

It was foolishness. He followed his cousin, reminding himself as he caught up to Kaden's long strides that Piper had come with them of her own desire and would return to the future with Kaden and Anna just as soon as she was able.

She was not his responsibility, nor was he fool enough to think she would wish to be.

"I did not expect to see any of this again," Kaden confessed as they walked the well-worn road leading to the village.

He could not help but voice his curiosity. "And did the thought please ye? Were ye glad to be rid of all of us?"

Kaden rolled his eyes, shoving his cousin in a playful manner. "Ye know that is not so. I would never be glad to be rid of ye."

"Forgive me for the asking, then, but what made it so easy for ye to choose the future?"

He wondered if it should have surprised him that his cousin did not need to give this much thought before he answered.

"Because she is the future. My future. I was given a choice to either stay here or follow her. From what she had told me of her time, it seemed a frightful place."

Aidan held his tongue, although he fully agreed with this after having seen the place himself.

"And I suspect I might have escaped the men quickly enough. I might have mounted Kirk's horse and fled. His is the swiftest beast on four hooves, as we all know. Yet I could not bring myself to do it. She was leaving, I would never see her again, and at that moment as in every moment since she was all that meant anything. Even if I managed to secure my freedom, what good would it do me if it left me without her?"

"I do wish ye had believed ye might speak to me of this," Aidan confessed. "Of your feelings toward her, ye ken. I was unaware of ye taking such a liking to her."

"More than a liking, though I know well what you mean. That was the purpose of my remaining silent. It was to protect her, for Kirk and those who follow him without thinking might have blamed her for bewitching me or something of the sort. I would not have that. It was of great importance to pretend she meant nothing to me."

"Ye did admirably well."

Kaden chuckled darkly. "Not quite so admirably well, for Kirk saw through me."

"What shall we do, then? Find horses, ride to your mother's. What will we do then?"

Kaden shook his head. "I have not thought so far ahead, I must admit. Warn her, for certain. She ought to stay far away from Kirk MacGregor. Perhaps there is somewhere else she might live now. After all, I will no longer be here."

"I will."

Kaden grinned. "Perhaps my pride was speaking for me. I did not mean to say I would not be here to look after her, but that I would no longer be here for her to remain near."

"Do ye believe ye are the only person who ever visited the woman?" Aidan might have boxed his cousin's ears. "To be sure, ye might have spent more time with the woman than ye did."

The surprise on Kaden's face was plain. "Are ye accusing me of being a poor son to the woman? For allow me to assure ye, I have blamed myself since the moment I held her dying body in my arms. Ye need not point out my flaws to me, cousin."

That had been a misstep. Aidan knew better than to speak in such a way without thinking, even to his cousin. There were times when the man was so unaware as to be blind. "What I mean to say is, I have seen her many times. My father has sent items to her, supplies. I have spent many afternoons at her fire."

Kaden stopped, staring. "Ye canna mean it. How was I not aware of this?"

"Do ye expect me to be aware of everything ye have done in the years since my father took ye from your mother's home for your protection? Was I to stop seeing her as I once did when we were lads? Ye must remember those times."

"Fondly. But it was a great danger to ye as a man."

Aidan lifted his shoulder. "Not such a danger that it was worth abandoning her. Not that ye abandoned her, ye ken. Ye have always been a good son. Why would ye have come back here otherwise? Ye knew not what ye would arrive to find, yet ye came back to spare her. That is a fine thing."

Even so, Kaden walked in pensive silence, which Aidan supposed was a sign of his new confusion. Men such as himself did not take well to finding their world was not precisely as they had imagined it.

The fact was, Aidan had kept his visits to Isla secret for the same reason Kaden would've done. It was a terrible crime to see a witch for any reason, even if that reason was for nothing other than paying a call and seeing to the witch's well-being.

She had read his future once, or had enjoyed pretending to do so. Though years had passed since that cold, damp day by her fire, he had never forgotten her speaking of a woman destined to enter his life from far, far away. She had been quite insistent on this as she read the leaves at the bottom of his cup once he had finished his tea.

He turned his attention to the familiar sights around him, his soul all but singing. None of those shining carts, or the stone-covered roads and walkways. None of the leering lads who had simply invited him to bury his sword to the hilt in their laughing faces. None of the noises, none of the stench.

Though he had found the young women worth noticing. He would miss the sight of them walking so brazenly down the street while wearing next to nothing.

"Imagine what the rest of them would think if they knew what we know." He looked to Kaden with a wry grin. "What would they say? What would they think?"

Kaden laughed, albeit with an edge. "Ye would just as well keep those thoughts to yourself, cousin. Unless ye wish to be accused of witchcraft yourself."

Aidan chuckled, seeing the humor in this, but Kaden's warning sent a cold chill to his heart. It was true, he would certainly be dismissed if anyone ever heard him speak of the things he had seen during that terrible time.

Dismissal would be the best result, in fact. They would dismiss him if he were fortunate.

Were he not fortunate, they would indeed determine him to have consorted with a witch or to be under the thrall of one. That would not end so well for him.

"I must keep this to myself until my dying day," Aidan mused aloud.

"Aye, ye must. Do ye believe ye can?"

There was no doubt. "Aye. In fact, I would wish to forget it. Except for ye. I am certain there will be times I will think of ye and ask myself how ye are faring in the world."

"And I shall do the same for ye," Kaden agreed. "Perhaps Anna and I will name our first son after ye."

Of course, these were empty words. Aidan would never know what became of his cousin, just as Kaden would never know what had become of him. And Aidan would have to keep his disappearance secret for always, never able to tell another living soul what had become of the man who had once seemed to be the future of Clan MacGregor.

Kirk McGregor rode up to meet them, his face a mask of stormy impatience. He had never been a man who enjoyed waiting. "There ye are. Clyde told me you were to join us, yet ye kept me waiting for far too long."

Kaden's sharp intake of breath spoke of the folly of the plan they had put together so quickly. For all Kaden saw now was the man who had murdered his mother.

Even though that murder had not yet taken place.

11

———

"I swear, I can still smell them." Piper wrinkled her nose in disgust at the memory of the men whose scent still lingered in the air. "I can't believe you survived weeks of this."

"Tell me about it." Anna sat cross-legged on the ground, her back to a tree. "It was pretty bad when they just came riding back. I remember that more clearly than anything else. They had just been out in the Highlands for weeks. I guess they never came across, you know, a stream they could dip themselves into."

"Even if they had, they wouldn't have used soap."

Anna tipped her head to the side at this. "Eh. Honestly, I think if you've never used what we use as soap, you don't really need it. I mean, once they take a swim or whatever, they're okay. Of course, they rarely do and then put the same dirty clothes back on, but…"

"Ugh. Enough, please. I don't know if I can stomach much more."

"Hey, you're the one who was all jazzed up about

coming to the past." Anna winked. "Now you know what it was really all about. Stinkiness and dirtiness and being gross."

"And their hands were so filthy!"

"Yup. No wonder they all died so young." Her voice caught, and she wasn't joking anymore. She looked at the ground, her mouth curving downward. "Wow. That sucks."

Piper knelt next to her. "You don't have to feel bad. It's easy to forget when you see them in person, but these people aren't alive anymore. Not in our time. But they seem happy enough now, right?"

Anna snorted. "You realize I love one of them, right? And he happens to be here right now, in his own time. Which by the way, scares him a hell of a lot less than our time does. And he could easily decide he doesn't wanna come back with me."

"He would never!"

"You don't know he'll wanna come back. You don't. Even I don't." She rubbed her arms, shivering. "He came through on a whim. Like a last second decision. I wouldn't ever make him stay with me if he wanted to go back. I couldn't do that to him. So now I just have to hope he loves me enough to want to make the same choice again. No big deal."

"Have you seen the way he looks at you? Like, seriously?"

"How does he look at me?"

"Like he's in the middle of the ocean and you're a life raft."

"Yeah, but it's not such a scary ocean when he's here. He can take care of himself here."

"Why did he look at you that way before he left with Aidan, then? Because he did. He so did. I felt like maybe I shouldn't be around for it."

This got Anna to laugh a little. "Okay. I get it."

"He'll come with you. I'm sure he will." She couldn't help but sigh. "It's amazing when you think about it. What if that's the whole reason you went to the past? To find him? Finding him wasn't a coincidence. It was the purpose."

"You think so?"

"God, I hope so. Otherwise, we really do live in a completely random universe, and anything could happen at any time."

"Good point."

She couldn't help herself. "When did you know you... I mean, when did you figure out you..."

"Loved him?" Anna closed her eyes, tipping her head back so it rested against the tree trunk. "I don't remember. Honestly, I don't think there was any single moment when I was like, yes, I love this man. It happened over time. He was good to me. Not always, not at first, though I think he was mean because he wanted to keep me safe. He knew if I didn't play along and be quiet and docile, I'd get myself killed. I figured he was right pretty fast, thank God. Once I figured out that I wasn't dreaming or sick or in the middle of a live action role play game."

"Oh, my God," Piper laughed. "That's what you thought?"

Anna shrugged. "Gee. What would you think if you opened your eyes and those guys came riding up to you out of nowhere? All stinky and whatnot?"

"Yeah. I guess you have a point."

"There was nobody to tell me I was in the sixteen hundreds. I had to wait for Kaden to tell me later on. And even then, I thought I was dreaming for a while. It wasn't exactly the easiest thing to accept."

"I understand that. I wouldn't have believed Aidan if he hadn't shown me what was in his pouch."

"Is that a euphemism?" Anna snickered.

"Shut up! His pouch, like his purse or whatever you wanna call it. I asked to look inside. When I found the coins from this time, I started to believe him. That and the sword and the complete lack of awareness of even the basics of modern life convinced me."

"Did he ask you how people got into the TV?"

"What do you think?"

They laughed softly, still careful not to announce their presence. She didn't want to imagine what would happen to them if they were found.

One witch all by herself was bad enough. Two witches were practically a coven.

There was nothing else to do but ask questions. It was either talk or sit and think and worry. Anna was obviously worried about Kaden; she kept rocking back and forth, slightly but obviously. "What do you think you'll do? Buy him a plane ticket and take him home with you?" Piper asked, trying to steer her brain away from worrying.

But that was the last thing she should've asked if she wanted to make her friend stop worrying.

"Oh, my gosh, I never thought about it. Shoot! What's he going to do? He's gonna freak out, that's what he's gonna do."

"Okay, okay. Sorry. I shouldn't have said anything.

Maybe you don't have to go back as soon as you thought you did."

"No, because I have to get back to Dad, eventually. I feel bad enough being away from him for this long."

"That's what nurses are for," Piper whispered. She knew enough about Anna's situation that she felt like she could speak up. Though not enough that she felt comfortable saying much more than what she hoped would encourage her friend. "You can't take everything on yourself. You're already out here, busting your butt, going to meetings, trying to get signed. All so you can afford to take care of him. I don't see your sister doing that."

It was a tricky sort of thing to say, and she hoped Anna wouldn't take it the wrong way. If there was one thing Piper couldn't stand, it was people who walked away from family when they needed help.

Maybe that came from knowing how it felt to get walked away from.

Anna sighed, but it was clear she got the message. "You're right. And it's not like we're losing any time by being here right now. When we go back, we won't have lost any time at all."

Piper hoped this was true, and she knew better than to voice her doubts. That would be just one more thing for Anna to worry about.

The thing was, there was no guarantee they'd get back to the same time as before.

"I have to try something." She stood, brushing the dirt and needles from her jeans. "Do you trust me?"

"What?" Anna scrambled to her feet. "No. Whatever it is

you're thinking, no. You can't leave this spot. It's too dangerous out there."

"I'm not going far, and you'll be able to see me the whole time. But you have to trust me, okay? Please. I have a theory about this and if I thought I was wrong, I wouldn't try it at all."

"What are you doing? You can't, whatever it is."

Piper held out her hand. "Let me see the rune."

"No way."

"Anna, come on. I don't want to have to fight you for it, but I wanna see how it works. Like I said, I think I have it worked out in my head. But I need to test it out so we can be sure."

"I don't like this." Anna's hand wandered down to the front pocket of her jeans, where she must have stashed the stone.

"I don't like it, either, but I really do think it'll be okay. It makes perfect sense."

"What does?" Anna hissed, looking out toward the road and the henge beyond like she was checking to make sure they weren't overheard.

"Look." Piper took a deep breath. "We have to test whether we'll get back to the same time, right? I think it makes sense that one of us should go through to see where we end up, then come through again."

"No! Because what happens if you can't get back through? Or you end up in another time when you come back? What if you don't come back to me?"

"I was never going to stay anyway."

"But you'll have the rune! And you'll have to keep it if

you wanna come back." Anna frowned. "Do you wanna come back?"

Oh, boy, it would've been easy to say no, that she didn't ever want to see this place again except in her own time. Sure, it was pretty and peaceful when the men wearing swords and crossbows weren't riding through. But she would've have stayed there permanently for all the money in the world.

"Yes, I'll come back. Of course, I will. If I don't, the whole purpose of the experiment will be null and void."

"I still don't understand the purpose," Anna admitted. "Why take a chance?"

"So you won't have to worry anymore," Piper explained. It wasn't easy to be patient when all she wanted to do was get it over with already. Now that she had made up her mind, she wanted to go through with it rather than worrying and wondering.

"And what if you don't come back to this time? We'll be stuck without the rune."

"See, that's what got me thinking in the first place. I've been turning it over in my head all along, ever since we got here and you weren't here. The you who first met Kaden, I mean. Everything went back to being the way it was before you showed up. Right?"

"Yeah."

"Okay. Then it stands to reason that Kaden's mom will have the rune when you find her. Right? Because it won't be here in this time anymore."

Anna blinked. "Now you've lost me."

"I'm pretty sure the same people or things can't exist in

the same time. I know, it's weird, but hear me out. Notice how Kaden and Aidan weren't with the group anymore. Aidan's dad was confused about it, obviously, because they had been riding with the group before we came through the stone. Then, all of a sudden, they ended up in front of the group instead of riding behind it. The versions of themselves that used to exist here vanished the second they showed up with us. But there was another version of them here already, before we got here. Which tells me there was another version of the rune here. I mean, if time keeps repeating over itself like it seems to do, Kaden's mom will have the same rune in her possession if I take this one through with me and can't come back. All you have to do is find her and get it."

Anna nodded slowly, frowning. "I get what you're saying, but it's still risky. You might not go back to the right time, did you ever think of that?"

"Yeah, no kidding, but thanks for the reminder. Listen. I'm willing to do this. I do believe it will work. If I didn't, I wouldn't take a chance. But isn't it better if we know how this works before we try to step through again? We could be walking through to any time at all. Heck, we might end up with dinosaurs all around us. Woolly mammoths or whatever."

Anna snorted. "I think you'd have to go to a time when the stones were standing here. That might rule out dinosaurs."

"Thank God for that," Piper muttered. "Come on. Hand it over. I'll do it. You'll see. It'll work."

"I don't like this."

"Yeah, well, I didn't ask if you like it or not. Come on.

Let's get it over with before the guys come back." She held out her hand, palm up. "Gimme."

"He's going to be so mad at me for letting you do this," Anna whispered as she fished the rune from her pocket.

"What is he, your daddy? No, he's not. You're not one of these seventeenth-century chicks. You can think for yourself."

Anna placed the rune in her palm. It felt like an ordinary stone. Nothing special. She tested its weight, examined the carving.

She then looked out to the road, making sure there was nobody coming. She would've heard a horse approach, but maybe not a person on foot. It seemed clear, so she darted out from inside the tree line and across the dirt road.

"Be careful!" Anna whispered from behind her. She was too nervous to step foot out in the open. Piper guessed she'd feel the same way if she had been through what was described. Iron shackles and peeing in a bucket in a horse pen, not to mention the way that pig Kirk had tried to torture her into doing his bidding.

Funny how the rune felt heavier the closer she got to the stone. It was all in her head, obviously. Just her subconscious freaking her out. Or so she told herself.

Just get it over with. This was your big idea. She looked up at the stone, which definitely seemed taller and sharper around the edges than it had before. Of course, because so many years of wind and rain had chipped away at it by the time she'd first seen it in the twenty-first century. Amazing.

She could do this. She had to try. What had Aidan done? He'd touched his hand to the stone while holding the rune. No big deal. She could handle it. She'd already come through time once, and it hadn't been any more diffi-cult than blinking an eye.

Still, she closed her eyes before reaching for the stone. Just because it had been easy to do before didn't mean she had to be happy about it.

This was it. Now or never.

She took a deep breath.

"We were on our way to ye," Aidan explained to the mounted chieftain when it was clear his cousin could not explain. Never had he expected to see the man again. At least, not alive, not in the saddle and glowering down at the two of them with his normal expression of disdain.

"What kept ye?" Kirk demanded, utterly unaware of what the two of them had been through or that they had both seen his dead body at some time. Aidan knew, of course, that he could give no indication of anything which had passed.

"Our mounts went lame," Aidan explained, the excuse pouring from his mouth before he had time to think it. It was as good an excuse as any, he supposed. "We came the rest of the way on foot."

Kaden merely stared up at the man, silent.

Kirk was far too concerned with other matters to give this much thought, waving a dismissive hand as he stared into the distance. He had like as not already forgotten why he was angry with the pair of them. He was that sort of man, one with far too many concerns to remain interested in one for very long.

And at that time, he would be most concerned with Clan Fraser. "Your father tells me what we might expect from the Frasers," Kirk barked. "As ever, he wishes me to speak to Malcolm Fraser and seek peace. Tell me, how is it that he fathered ye when he is less than half a man?"

Aidan's upper lip curled in a snarl before he could hold back. How much of a delight would it have been to tell him he was about to die? That he only had days left in his wicked life and had best make amends for his many sins?

It was Kaden who spoke, having gotten control of himself. "Clyde MacGregor only wishes to avoid costly battle if possible. Is it worth losing good men simply because ye cannot bring yourself to speak to the man? What about the women and children who will have to live with no one to care for them if their husband or their father is killed in a battle which might have been avoided?"

Kirk's jaw worked, tightening dangerously before he exploded. "I will care for them! It is I who decides what Clan MacGregor will and will not do, and it is I who bears the responsibility. This is how it has always been, though lads as young as yourself might not recall."

Kaden growled and spoke in spite of Aidan's warning hand on his arm. "Dinna call me a lad," he warned. "Ye were not speaking to me so when last we defended this land, were ye? Nay, because ye know me to be a fair man and true. And were it not for me, your men would not be half as prepared now. If there is a victory over Malcolm Fraser and his men, it will be because of myself."

Deep in the back of his mind, Aidan felt there was something terribly wrong with this. While it mattered little what Kaden said to the clan chieftain, as he and Anna would be on their way through the standing stone as soon as they found his mother, there were still dangers aplenty all around them.

Not only from Kirk MacGregor but from those who followed him blindly, hanging on his every word. They did not take well to hearing their leader disparaged or challenged in any way. And it was all too easy for him to have them do his fighting.

Little good would it do any of them if Kaden got himself killed before he was able to escape back to Anna's time.

"That is enough," Aidan barked, glaring at his cousin in hopes of getting through his head. "Ye must not allow fatigue to get the better of ye." He looked up at Kirk, whose face was a shade of red that could only mean danger. "It has been a trying fortnight," he explained with a shrug. "And today was the most difficult of all. We are both past exhaustion after losing the horses. Ye must forgive him."

Kirk spat upon the ground to show them both what he thought about Aidan's excuses. "Who are ye to tell me what I must do?"

There was no speaking to the man. He took everything as an insult. "Dinna mistake me, please. It would be best if we went to our homes and slept for the first time in days."

Kirk scoffed but did not protest. "Be gone with ye, then. I shall speak to ye at supper. Dinna disappoint me by failing to appear." He brought his horse about and trotted away, muttering to himself all the while. He was not a man skilled at concealing his anger.

"I shall kill him again," Kaden growled low enough that only Aidan could hear it. At least, Aidan hoped no one else could hear. All it would take was one person to claim they'd heard a threat against the MacGregor.

The village was a busy place as ever, and them in the center of it. Yet those walking past or riding or driving teams of cattle paid little attention to that which was no concern of theirs. For once, it seemed fortune was on their side.

Even so, this could not go on. "Watch what ye say," Aidan urged. "Ye must control your anger, man. If only for Anna's sake. And we must both keep cool heads if we are to find a way around this. How can we avoid meeting with the men during supper? If we dinna appear, he shall send guards to search for us. They might find the women."

As Aidan spoke, Kaden's eyes burned with murderous fire, nostrils flaring and mouth quivering. Aidan squeezed his shoulder as hard as he could and lowered his voice further but allowed a hard edge to shine through. "Remember. In this time, he has done nothing to ye. Not to ye, not to your mother. Ye must remember this. Ye must treat him as ye would had that never occurred."

"The smug, preening, self-important—"

"I know, but ye must forget it now. Or put it aside. Do what must be done that we might be successful now."

"We cannot linger until supper," Kaden mused, his senses returning to him as he heeded Aidan's warning. He no longer breathed like a wild stallion, and his eyes no longer flashed in warning. "What do we do with the lasses?"

"I could not say. The cottage is too far to make the ride

back and forth. If it were, I would suggest we send the lasses to your mother, as they would be safer there. But they could not make the ride on their own."

"Nay, I would not trust it. I would not have the two of them riding alone. Who is to say what might happen if they are discovered? I am certain whoever did the discovering would not be forgiving."

Aidan shuddered at the thought. It had been difficult enough for Anna. Two strange women would arouse double the suspicion. "I suppose there's nothing to do but wait. We might find a safer place for them to hide outside the village—anyone might ride past the henge."

"What ails the pair of ye?" Clyde McGregor looked and sounded as though he might wish to knock their heads together, as he had done so many times when they were lads. He walked his mount down the road running through the center of the village, his expression thunderous. "The MacGregor was looking for ye."

He dismounted, taking his course by the reins and glaring at them. "If I didna know better, I would think the two of ye were up to some devilry."

Aidan's heart swelled with love for his father. Even now, with the man in a terrible temper, just the sight of him went a long way toward erasing the confusion and helplessness he had suffered after finding himself in a foreign world. "We saw him," he explained.

"Aye, and he had quite a bit to say about yourself," Kaden added. He did what he could to speak more easily, with less anger than he had toward Kirk, though there remained a great deal of bitterness toward their chieftain. Aidan knew this was due to Kaden's fondness for Clyde.

He'd always resented Kirk's way of speaking down to him as if he were someone to be pushed about.

Clyde grumbled but allowed it to pass as ever he did. "Och, that is nothing new. He wishes to discuss strategy this evening. Ye had best make yourself seen there, or we will all have hell to pay."

What choice did they have? "Aye, we shall both be there," Aidan assured his father. "Ye had best return home to Mam before she searches the village for ye."

There was at last humor in Clyde's eye. "Tis I who have been searching for her, ye might rest assured." He chuckled to himself, leading the horse further down the road in search of his wife after weeks spent apart.

Aidan grimaced. "I suppose 'tis just as well I had no intention of returning to the house yet."

"We must return to the women. They will ask themselves where we are and perhaps think the worst." Kaden stroked his chin. "And we ought to secure horses. If they have need to flee, it would be best to do it in the saddle."

"They will not need to," Aidan reminded him as they walked down the road a bit further, to the stables where horses were kept should there be sudden need of them. If patrol guards were to come at full gallop and need fresh mounts to continue on, for example. "They have the rune. They can go through and be safe in their time."

Kaden said nothing.

His silence struck Aidan as rather ominous. "Can they not?" he prompted when his cousin offered no reply.

"What if she leaves and canna return?" he muttered. "I would have her be safe first, mind ye, and would tell her to go at the first sign of danger. Tis why I gave her the rune should she need to flee. But…" He looked pained.

"Aye. I ken what ye say, man. Ye need not say more." It was too difficult for Kaden to put into words, and Aidan thought he understood in a sense. His cousin loved the lass more than anything else in life and would die if it meant protecting her, but he did not have to be delighted at the thought of losing her forever.

"Dinna speak to her of this," Kaden warned. "I beg ye. I would not have her linger for my sake."

"Who do ye think ye speak to, man?" Aidan scoffed. "Am I such a fool in your eyes?"

"Nay, nay," Kaden grumbled, shaking his head. "Ye would ken better if ye knew what it meant to love someone so much more than yourself or anything, anyone else. Torn between wishing what is best for them and wishing nothing more than to be with them, always."

No, Aidan had never known what it meant, and when he witnessed the torment plaguing his cousin was relieved that he had never loved. What was the purpose of it if a man were so unhappy as a result?

They secured a pair of horses and took off for the henge. It would not be a long ride, and Aidan was grateful to be on horseback again. This was where he belonged, not in some flashing, shining cart which required the work of neither man nor beast to pull it. This was where he would more than gladly spend the rest of his days.

Though the notion of living out the rest of his life without his cousin did weigh heavily. "I shall miss having ye with us," he admitted while it was still only the pair of them. These were the sorts of thoughts a man did not wish to share while in the presence of women or anyone else. There might not be another time for him to say that which was in his heart.

"Aye," Kaden grunted, looking ahead. "I shall miss ye as well. And your da. I owe him my life, ye ken, and well I know it. I canna share this with him with no way to explain why I would say farewell. Ye might tell him what I said later. After."

"I shall," Aidan vowed. Just when that time would come was a mystery, but he would make certain of it.

They rode in silence after that, for what else was there to say? They were not the sort to share feelings easily. Not as the men in the TV did while Aidan watched. Did all men of the future share their hearts so freely? Practically weeping at a woman's feet in an effort to make her understand him.

The henge loomed ahead, reminding Aidan of what he had just endured and what his cousin would endure again. All for the sake of a woman.

"What is she on about?" Kaden muttered, nodding ahead. Where a slight, hooded figure darted from the woods and crossed the road.

"Damn her," Aidan muttered, already urging the horse to greater speed that he might catch Piper before she did anything truly foolish. Had she not been commanded to remain hidden? Why would she show herself this way?

She was reaching for the center stone, her other fist clenched.

He had ever been a man who listened to instinct when it came to important matters. His inner wisdom had never taken him in the wrong direction.

Which was why he knew without a doubt that in that clenched fist was the rune, and that she intended to go through.

Without even saying goodbye. The notion made his breath catch, made his heart clench. She was leaving without so much as a goodbye.

"What do ye think you're on about?" he demanded, startling her so that she jumped and released the rune. It fell to the ground at her feet.

He dismounted and took her by the arms, shaking her before he had the chance to stop himself. She was about to leave, the cruel thing, and he would never have seen her again. Her dark eyes were filled with fear as she looked up at him, her mouth half-open.

"Well?" he demanded, towering over her much smaller form. "Answer me!"

13

———

"Leave it off, man!" Kaden pulled Aidan away from Piper.

She was convinced that if he hadn't stepped in when he did, she might've been a goner.

The nice, sweet, protective guy she knew earlier had turned into a ragey piece of garbage. All it took was a little time back in his own world.

Good thing he was staying there, then. And to think, she had gone out of her way for him and even felt sorry for him more than once.

Kaden placed an arm around her shoulders and hurried her back to Anna, into the trees.

"She was only—" Anna began, but Kaden held a finger to his lips.

"There will be time for that. Wait." He went out again to get his horse and lead it into the woods. He was shaking his head, muttering to himself, but Piper didn't care too much about that. He was a decent guy, and he had kept her from getting her head taken off by a raging Highlander.

She cared more about that Highlander, standing by the center stone with his back turned to them. To call him a jerk would be an insult to jerks. Who did he think he was, putting his hands on her like that? Not to mention practically screaming in her face. The only thing keeping her from marching out there to smack him around a little was the fear of being caught by somebody else.

Or so she told herself.

He crouched and picked something up off the ground. She winced at the sight of the rune and knew he would give her a hard time about dropping it. She wouldn't have dropped it if he hadn't scared her half to death, but something told her he wouldn't care much about her excuses.

"I was trying to test a theory," Piper hissed. She didn't care if Kaden thought she should be quiet. She was never very good at getting yelled at for things that weren't her fault. Who was?

"What does that mean?" Kaden asked.

Anna explained it to him in a soft voice while Piper waited for Aidan to join them. He still had his back turned on them and the way his shoulders rose and fell told her he was breathing heavily. What was his issue?

"That was a great risk ye were about to take, lass," Kaden announced in a defeated voice. "Truly. Tis glad I am we came upon ye when we did."

"Why?" she challenged. "Are you gonna give me a hard time now, too?"

"Nay, nay," he replied. "I would not dream of it."

"I wasn't trying to leave you here with no way to get back," she explained. Why did she feel so guilty? She hadn't done anything wrong, and she hadn't even gone through with her plan. "Besides, he doesn't even wanna go back. Why was he so angry?"

"Ye would have to ask him."

"Yeah, well, that's not gonna happen now that he put his hands on me. He didn't have any right to do that. I don't care what century we're in. That's not cool."

"Verra well," he agreed. "I shall speak to him of it. While I do, ye must remain here. Do ye ken? Here. Where none can see ye."

She nodded without offering any argument. He seemed like he was in a mood, and she didn't need two Highlanders on her case. One was bad enough.

Anna gave her a hug. "I'm glad he stopped you before you went through with it," she confessed. "I was really scared."

"I told you, I would—"

Anna shook her head. "That's not it. At least, that's not all of it. I was afraid we would end up in different times, or timelines. This is all so confusing. Maybe it's not a good idea for us to experiment with it. At least if we go together, we'll be together in the same time when we arrive wherever we arrive. But it would make me really sad if I ended up without you."

This took Piper by surprise. Her breath caught in her throat, her eyes welling up with unexpected tears. She had never imagined Anna saying anything like that. They were friends, and they had worked hard to get their band where they wanted to be. Two chicks against the world, they used to call themselves. A pair of girls trying to be taken seriously in an industry where no matter how many strides had been made by women, men still tried to take advantage of those they saw as easy targets.

Even though they had been through all this together, Piper wouldn't have called them close friends. Good friends, maybe. But not close. Maybe that was just the way she saw it, though. Maybe Anna saw it differently all along.

One of the many pitfalls of never having a normal family, she guessed. She was never very good at making friends and even worse at keeping them.

If anybody ever took the time to ask her the most important thing a kid could learn when they were growing up, she would tell them flat-out that a kid needed to know they were worth knowing, worth loving, worth caring about. Not for any other reason than the fact that they lived and breathed air. Not for what they could do for other people or for how much they had. Just for themselves.

"Yeah. I would be sad if I ended up without you, too." Maybe it had been a crazy theory, and maybe she had been a little too quick to want to test it out. And maybe it had been for the best that Aidan had caught her before she went through.

But that still didn't give him an excuse to grab her the way he had. He might not have meant to hurt her, and it didn't hurt. Not really. But she still felt his hands on her arms, even though minutes had passed. Sort of a dull, thumping pressure.

She held her breath as he crossed the road, taking his horse by the reins and leading it. She had never been so close to a horse before in her life and wasn't a fan, but she wouldn't let him know this for anything in the world. He would probably look down on her.

He grimaced, his jaw tightening and loosening, his mouth drawing into a thin line. When he spoke, his words were slow and halting, his voice gruff. "I should not have reacted as I did. I saw ye and believed ye were taking the rune and leaving Anna and Kaden stranded here when they did not wish to be. I didna think before I acted. I ask for your forgiveness." He sort of choked that last part out, like it hurt to apologize.

"I wouldn't leave them here! What is wrong with you? I know they want to go back. Do you think I'm that kind of person? I mean, after everything we went through and the grief you put me through while we were out in public and I was trying to make sure you didn't get arrested—"

"As I said, I didna think. Could ye not hear?"

Anna stepped between them. "All right, all right. Aidan said he was sorry, and Piper was only trying to do what she thought was best for everybody. We have to let it go now. There are so many other things for us to worry about."

That hardly cleared things up for Piper. She glared at Aidan over the top of Anna's head.

"What did you find in the village?" Anna asked Kaden. "Can we get moving?"

He sighed. "Nay. Not yet. I must ask that ye remain here for now."

"Kirk expects us at supper," Aidan explained in a tight voice. "If we dinna appear, he will like as not send men after us. We canna risk them finding ye."

Great. Another reason to spend more time in the middle of nowhere and with nothing to eat. This was looking like a worse idea with every passing minute.

"We ought to have brought ye food," Aidan observed

with a groan, like he could read her thoughts. Or maybe he could hear the rumbling of her stomach. "We shall bring something to eat when we return from supper."

"Won't it be dark by then? And late? Are we going to ride out to the cottage afterward?"

"It might be best to wait until morning to do that," Kaden reasoned. "Tis a lengthy journey through dense wood. We need all the light available to us."

"Where we could stay the night, then?" Piper asked, looking around.

Aidan snickered. "Perhaps the nearest hotel?"

That was a mistake. She turned to him, her fists clenching. "Don't make fun of me," she warned. "I was only asking."

"We'll stay out here. Deeper in the woods, of course, but that's all we can do. It'll be like camping." Anna was doing her best to put a positive spin on things, and Piper had to give her credit for that.

That didn't mean she had to be happy about it. "I've never been camping," she admitted.

"What is camping?" Kaden asked before shaking his head. "Never ye mind. I've the feeling it would be beyond my ken."

Nevertheless, Anna explained. "It's when people go out into nature and sleep outside. They have tents, fires, that sort of thing."

"Ye mean to say, people in your time dinna wish to sleep indoors and so choose places where they might sleep out-of-doors?" Aidan asked, his brows drawing together. "That might be the thing I understand least. Why would anyone choose to sleep in the out of doors when they might do so in comfort and warmth?"

"And away from the rain?" Kaden added. "I am a man who prefers being in the out of doors, but sleeping among the animals and ever having an ear open to their sounds—"

"Wow. You're making me feel a lot better about this," Piper muttered, looking from one of them to the other. "Honestly. I was already super looking forward to it, but you're taking my excitement over the top. Thanks for that."

"Ye will not be alone," Aidan assured her.

"That makes me feel a lot better," she grunted, remembering the hands on her arms and how rude he'd been. How he had come just short of screaming in her face.

"Hey. Enough." Anna gave her a look that brought to mind the nuns at the Catholic school she'd attended for a few years. A look that meant a person would be pretty stupid to keep talking. Funny how that look translated even when a person wasn't wearing a habit.

"We shall start at first light, most certainly. Dinna ye fret."

Aidan was doing everything he could to warm her up again, and it wasn't working. He could fall off the face of the earth, as far as she was concerned.

14

"I have the strangest feeling that I have done this before," Kaden murmured as they took their places at the table.

"Because ye have?" Aidan asked in a low voice, eyes moving around the room. It seemed there were possible threats everywhere, though these men were the same men he'd known his entire life. There was no reason for any of them to pose a threat.

It was guilt. It was knowing that he knew something none of them understood. None of them would ever understand, for he hardly understood it himself.

If they found he had somehow visited another time, they would condemn him. They would lock him away in a cell there would be no escape from. Or he would be killed, quickly and without a second thought.

This made them enemies. He told himself they were not, and that he could not think of them this way, but there was no helping it. He had a secret, and he had never been a good man with a secret.

He could never avoid suspecting everyone knew what he knew. Or dreading it.

Kirk was in a temper, as ever, with his ire directed at Clyde. As ever. "Ye canna mean it. Ye canna. Not when Malcolm Fraser makes a point of marching on any territory he believes he can claim for his own. Ye would have me speak to the man as if he were nothing more than a man, one able to reason."

Aidan's father opened his mouth to speak, but it was Kaden who spoke instead. "Malcolm Fraser is not a man to easily listen to reason, as ye say, but Clyde makes a strong point. He does not deserve to be treated so."

"Ye have no place speaking to me as ye do," Kirk warned, his voice a deep growl.

"He merely wishes to spare the lives of our men until there is no choice but to battle," Aidan added.

Kirk raised a finger, pointing to Aidan. "And yourself, speaking on yer father's side. No matter what comes from the man's mouth, ye agree with him."

Aidan felt a flush rising over his throat, working its way up to his face. "He speaks sense." Kaden kicked him beneath the table as a warning, and Aidan understood why. His voice had already risen to dangerous levels, very nearly shouting at the clan's chieftain.

"Sense for a woman," Kirk spat.

Aidan's gaze fell upon his father, seated at the other side of the table. He bore Kirk's disdain as he always did, with a blank expression belying the rage boiling deep within him. Aidan knew this rage, had heard it expressed many times over the course of his years.

Clyde MacGregor was in most instances a fair, reasonable, thoughtful man who could easily turn into a vicious, mad dog when pushed to his limits. Kirk MacGregor knew exactly how to push him.

He never took his rage out upon his wife, his son or his nephew. That was not his way. But he would sometimes ride for hours at a time and scream into the open air, his head tipped back to face the sky. Aidan and Kaden had followed him once as lads, riding at a safe distance behind him and waiting in the woods.

They had never spoken of it, as this was not the sort of thing a man spoke of. But Aidan had never forgotten the manner in which his father's weathered face had flushed deep red, his clenched fists raised to the sky. The utter fury which Kirk MacGregor's careless words and dismissive ways had brought to life.

Aidan thought that if he had to name a certain moment in which he had first begun to question Kirk MacDougal's worthiness to serve as chieftain, it was that very moment. And the feeling had not left him as he had grown from youth to manhood. In fact, it had grown.

"If wishing to speak on behalf of peace makes my father a woman, then I am a woman as well," Aidan declared as he thumped a fist against the table. "For ye well know—as every man at this table and around this room knows—that Clyde MacGregor will ride at the front of the line when the time comes to face the enemy on the field of battle. He has proven himself time and again."

Rather than thanking him for his support, his father looked rather shocked and perhaps despaired on behalf of his son. This was not a surprise. Perhaps he had spoken too soon or without thinking enough beforehand, but there was no holding himself back when the man insisted on insulting the greatest man Aidan had ever known.

Kirk drew several loud, long breaths. This was for the benefit of all around him, proof that he worked to call his temper under control. That he was not thoughtless nor callous. "I dinna recall asking for yer thoughts," he muttered.

"Nay, for ye knew I would speak against ye," Aidan muttered, which earned yet another strong kick from beneath the table. Harder this time, and more determined to cause him pain. To silence him.

Perhaps that was for the best. He had only just warned his cousin against thinking of Kirk as the man who had killed his mother. Yet here he was, challenging his chieftain and certainly making his existence in the clan difficult. And dangerous.

Kaden would not be there to support him and speak on his behalf for much longer. He would do well to keep that in mind. His cousin was the other voice of reason within the clan. Once he returned to Anna's time, there would be no one else with the courage or intelligence to think and speak for themselves.

"We will battle the Frasers," Kaden muttered. "That is how it must be. But ye canna discard an opinion which is not in agreement with your own simply because it is disagreement. It is good sense to seek peace first. I dinna wish to lose good men."

"As far as I can tell, that is yer doing," Kirk retorted. "For 'tis yourself who trains the men and sees to their worthiness." Yes, and there was no longer a witch to rely on. It was easy to forget how things had changed since the last time they had gone over this problem.

There was no Anna, so long as Kirk knew. No witch. Only his men. Yet Aidan had first assumed Kirk's eagerness to go to battle had everything to do with the witch he'd imagined having on his side.

Now, he knew the man simply wished to go to shed blood and send a message to any and all who wished to challenge his right to what was his. Aidan respected this. Truly, it was not Kirk's desire to fight which disgusted him.

It was the manner in which he treated those who would speak against rushing headlong into a foolhardy fight.

His father sent him a look of warning, and perhaps something more. Anger, perhaps. Aidan wished he could explain to the man what had come to pass. He felt that it was perhaps his father he wished most to tell.

It was only after they had eaten—from the small amount both he and Kaden had consumed, it seemed neither had much of an appetite—that Clyde managed to pull Aidan aside. "What do ye think ye are on about?" he demanded in a tight whisper.

"Ye know it pains me to hear him speak to ye in such a way." That was as much as he could say, as much as he trusted himself to speak. And it was the truth, fully and truly. "I believe it is time someone spoke for ye."

"I need no man to speak for me," his father growled. "I have been doing my speaking for longer than ye have been alive, lad, and ye would do well to remember that."

A mixture of righteous indignation and shame rose in Aidan's chest. It had never been easy for him to accept being scolded when he felt he was in the right. Now more than ever, he wished to be understood.

For he had already been greatly misunderstood earlier that day, something which he knew there would be no coming back from. Something which he could not make sense of no matter how he looked at it.

Precisely what had he been thinking when he frightened Piper?

He escaped with the mumbled apology, none of the words clear, but it was enough for his father who moved along in favor of speaking to old Fergus. Fergus was another man of sense, having sacrificed an eye for the clan during one of the battles they'd waged before Aidan was born. It was a comfort to know his father had someone to share his true thoughts with.

As for himself, there was no one with whom he might share the turmoil he'd struggled against all through the day. Ever since coming upon the standing stone and finding Piper moments from going through time, he'd turned the matter over in his mind, again and again, trying to make sense of the confusion and disappointment in himself.

For he had disappointed himself, quite badly. His heart clenched whenever he recalled the fear in Piper's eyes, the way she had quaked as he bellowed at her.

And why had he bellowed? Partly for the reason he had given. She might have been intending to leave Kaden and Anna behind, taking the rune with her.

That was only a small part of it. The rest had become clear in the moments after Kaden led her away, while he stood beside the stone and struggled to contain the helpless rage he'd knew he succumbed to.

He had thought she was about to leave him, and that had been enough to stir him into a frenzy. He had feared she had been on her way without exchanging even one more word with him. He would never see her again, never hear her voice, never watch her roll her eyes as he asked what to him was a perfectly reasonable question.

It was this which had given him pause, forcing him to think about what the lass meant to him. He still was uncertain, but what he knew without a doubt was that he had taken an interest in her far beyond the ordinary.

And it caused him no small bit of grief.

Kaden caught his eye across the room, and Aidan knew what this meant. They had to secure food for the women, who both of whom were unable to fend for themselves in this world. In the future, they would only use one of those devices of theirs to ask someone to bring them their next meal; he had seen the people in the TV do this time and again while Piper slept.

Little wonder men had nothing better to do with their time than torment lasses in the street.

One of the serving lasses passed his way, and he made a point of catching up to her and engaging her in trivial conversation. A comely thing, and quite interested in his attention. It had never been a difficult matter, securing the affection of a willing lass.

And just why did the knowing of it now cause him shame? Why did Piper's face flash before his eyes even as he looked upon a lass who was as different from her as night was from day?

No matter. Her favor meant his being able to take what was left of the roasted meat and potatoes, both of which he wrapped in linen before tucking them into a sack. Kaden had secured bread and ale, as per their plan.

How he wished it did not please him so, the notion of returning to the place in the woods where they had left the pair of women from the future.

How he wished she had not been on his mind throughout the hours they had spent apart.

15

"Well, damn."

Piper sat up, throwing her arms over her head and stretching. The first bits of light had already begun to peek through the tree branches overhead, and she was sure she had never smelled anything as sweet as the morning air on that particular day.

On top of that, she had slept like the dead. That night had easily been in the top five best night's sleep she had ever experienced. And there she had been, fretful and nervous and wondering if she should even close her eyes for fear of what might sneak up on her in the night.

Once sleep had hit her, it had hit her hard and not given up until the singing of birds she couldn't see stirred her from her dreams.

Now, she looked around from the relative comfort of the blanket beneath her and the saddle which she used as a pillow. That, she could've done without, but when a person was tired to the point of exhaustion, there wasn't much room for complaint.

Kaden and Anna were sleeping on the other side of what had been a fire but was now nothing more than burned-out embers.

But there was no Aidan.

He was probably taking care business behind a tree or something. Of course, she would have to do the same thing. Not something she looked forward to, but she wouldn't have to be there for much longer. According to Kaden, his mother's cottage was maybe a half-day's ride. They could be back in the future—the real world, as she saw it—by nightfall.

And she could take a shower, and she could put on clean clothes and sleep in the big, soft bed. She could order room service and watch TV or look at cat videos on her phone. Whatever she wanted to do, the entire world was at her fingertips.

She was smiling about this, imagining everything she wanted to do after her brief journey to the past, when she noticed Aidan still hadn't come back.

She got up, careful to quiet so she wouldn't wake the lovebirds, and wandered into the trees. She wouldn't go far —she wasn't crazy—but she couldn't stand the thought of not knowing where he was.

Had he abandoned them? She could imagine this. She could imagine him deciding this was all too much trouble —after all, he had gotten what he wanted out of the deal, hadn't he? He was back where he wanted to be, even if she couldn't imagine anybody wanted to be in this time or this place when they might benefit from technology and medicine and hygiene and...

"Aidan?" she whispered, moving from one tree to the

next but always careful to stay within range of Anna. "Where are you?"

A rustling in the brush nearby almost stopped her heart, and she laughed softly at herself when a squirrel came scurrying out. At least squirrels hadn't changed over the centuries.

No Aidan, though. The disgust and distrust that had started the day before were blossoming into outright hatred. He ran off and abandoned them! What kind of jerk did that?

Good, he could stay in the past. The past could have him.

Just as she thought this, an exposed root took her by surprise. She managed not to scream, but just barely, as her ankle turned and she landed on her hands and knees.

More rustling this time, louder than it had been before. Much louder. Somebody was coming, walking through the woods.

She now understood what an animal felt like when they knew they were trapped. Her heart beat hard enough to make her sick, her stomach churning. Somebody had found her, and they would lock her up the way Anna had been locked up, and they would think she was a witch. They would try to use her, or maybe they would kill her, yes, they would kill her. She could practically feel the noose around her neck, tightening until she could barely breathe.

Aidan found her gasping, clutching her throat. He crouched in front of her, holding by the rains the pair of horses he was leading. "Tis only myself, lass." The horses pranced around, digging at the soil with their hooves and sniffing her.

Somehow, that was even more horrifying than anything she had imagined in her panicked brain. She cringed, throwing an arm over her face. "Get them away!" she whispered.

He snickered rather than take her seriously. "Them? They are the gentlest creatures ye will ever meet."

"That's all fine and good for you to say, but they're still animals, and I still don't like them." She fought her way to her feet, testing her weight on her turned ankle. It was easier to look down at her ankle and check it for swelling than it was to look him in the eye.

She had been so sure he had abandoned them, and what happened? He stumbled upon her while she was making a fool of herself, scrambling around on her hands and knees.

"Can ye walk on it, lass?" he asked, and she was glad to hear no humor his voice. He wasn't making fun of her or laughing to himself over what an idiot she was.

"I think so. I don't think it was that bad." She brushed herself off, chuckling darkly at how scared she had made herself. "It's just that I thought you were somebody else. You know, a threat."

He made an understanding sort of noise. "Och, forgive me. I didna intend to startle ye."

"Where were you?" He didn't need to know she had been looking for him.

He looked to the horses, scratching one of them behind the ears. "I rode to the village to secure a mare for ye. I suspected Kaden and Anna would share Kaden's mount, but ye would need one of your own."

For a second, his thoughtfulness touched her. He didn't

need to go out of his way like that, and before the sun had even come up.

It was just a shame that horses scared her half to death.

She tried to be as dignified as possible. "Thank you, but... I don't know how to ride."

The funniest look came over his face then. First, he frowned deeply, his brows lowering to the point where she could barely see his eyes. Like she had just said something he absolutely could not make sense of.

That was before he burst out laughing. "Ye canna mean it."

She should've known he would be snotty. "Why not? Sorry, horseback riding isn't exactly something we learned in school. It's not required."

He waved a hand, still chuckling. "Dinna mistake me. I dinna mean to laugh at ye."

"You could've fooled me," she muttered, folding her arms.

"Riding a horse is no difficulty, lass. I assure ye. Ye need only sit in the saddle and direct the animal using the reins and the pressure of your knees. Tis nothing more than that."

Sure. Just like flying an airplane was nothing more than keeping it in the air. "Well, the thing is... I mean, besides the fact that you consider it easy because you've been doing your whole life, there's also the fact that horses scare me half to death. I mean, can't you tell?" She was practically climbing the tree, for God's sake, all in an effort to put distance between herself and the pair of horses Aidan still held onto.

"You're afraid of them? Why?"

It wasn't so much the question that bothered her. It was the way he asked it. "This from the man who was afraid to ride in a car," she snapped. "Sorry, but I wasn't lucky enough to be raised around horses, okay? They're big, they're strong, and I'm not used to them."

For that matter, she might as well have been talking about Aidan himself. She wasn't used to men like him.

At least she seemed to get through to him. Maybe it was the comment about him being afraid of the cars he had seen during his brief trip that got the point across. "I see. Ye might make yourself familiar with this mare while Kaden and Anna prepare themselves for the ride. She is quite gentle. I chose her with ye in mind," he confessed with what struck her as a shy smile.

Wasn't she supposed to hate him? Hadn't he terrified her, not to mention the fact that he put his hands on her without permission? But there she was, softening under that smile. She felt that happening, felt herself melting a little, and wished it wasn't so easy for him to get back in her good graces.

"You did?" she asked, her heart sinking and swelling at the same time. Now it would seem rude if she didn't at least try to get to know the horse. He had taken all the trouble of riding into the village and choosing the horse especially for her.

The least she could do was give it a shot.

She seemed like a sweet, old horse. Gentle. While Aidan's chestnut brown gelding—he had called it that, and she had tried to commit the word to memory just like he had tried to remember words like ambulance and hospital

—seemed a little pushy, a little insistent, her gray mare only sniffed softly at the sleeve of her hoodie.

"It's gray, just like you," she whispered, telling herself the horse meant no harm and was only exploring its surroundings. Just because it was much bigger than her and could probably crush her without meaning to didn't mean it wanted to crush her or even that it would.

"Take care, now. Animals can sense fear, and it makes them fearful." Aidan kept his distance but also kept watching, like he wanted to be sure nothing bad happened.

"Oh, great. Now I have even more to be nervous about."

He barely stifled a laugh. "Move slowly at first. No sudden movements, ye ken. Once she gets a sense of ye, and the ye of her, ye will both feel more comfortable with the other."

Somehow, that didn't make her feel better. She would try, only because he had gone out of his way for her.

"They dinna use horses in your time," Aidan murmured. "Ye might scratch her behind the ears. She will enjoy that."

"Which one of us are you talking to?" she muttered.

He chuckled at this but didn't answer. She scratched behind the horse's ears as he suggested. "How do I know if she likes it?"

"Let us say that ye would know if she did not," he replied with way too much humor for her liking.

"I'm glad you think this is so funny, I really am. Of course, I didn't force you to get into a car or anything, but who's keeping score? I'm not. And no, we don't use horses in my time as much as you use them here. Sure, people ride them. I guess they get used on farms and ranches and stuff. But I grew up in a place where there were only trees in the park, and the park was miles away. The only horses I ever saw were on TV or in movies."

"I assure ye, there is nothing to fear. They are just animals, like any other. Ye simply need to know how to behave around them, and it helps if you are the sort of person they like."

"What sort of person do they like?" she asked, finally daring to glance his way. It seemed like the mare was taking to her, accepting her scratches and pets without shying away.

"One who is patient. One who will not mistreat them, who will speak kindly to them and encourage them." He paused, then added, "One who would find a stranger in the rain and take him with them, who would see to their comfort and make certain they were not taken by the law for carrying a sword or threatening lads in the street. One who would take the time to explain things, so they would not be afraid. One would not force them to ride in one of those shiny cars that are so loud and smell so terribly. That sort of person."

Well, that was unfortunate.

Why did he have to go and say that? Why did he have to go and look at her the way he looked at her when she turned away from the mare to stare at him in surprise?

There was light shining in his eyes that had nothing to do with the sun. In fact, it was still pretty dark where they stood, but he seemed to glow from within. She couldn't take her eyes off him, especially when she went and remembered what he looked like wearing nothing but a towel, fresh from the shower.

It wasn't easy to think of that man and this man—the one who'd yelled at her, who brought back a hundred memories of other men who yelled—as being the same person. But he was, and she now understood that he had reacted before thinking. He had probably wanted nothing more than to make sure his cousin didn't get stranded in a time he didn't want to be in anymore.

"Oh, he brought another horse." Anna joined them, unaware of what she had missed. "I never thought I would see Piper so close to one. I thought you were terrified of them."

Piper nodded, still staring at Aidan. "Yeah, I thought I was, too. But I guess I was wrong."

She had been wrong about a lot of things.

16

———

"So, there's really no other version of me here at all right now?" Anna marveled, riding behind Kaden with her arms around his waist. "That's fascinating. It means there could be so many different timelines!"

"Fascinating," Piper mused, though the heaviness in her voice spoke of a darker take on the situation. "There's another version of you out there somewhere. The one you saw getting electrocuted just after you got back to our present time. I wonder what she's up to."

"I canna say I understand any of this," Aidan grunted with a frown.

"None of us do," Piper reminded him with a softer smile than any he had seen since their arrival in his time. "You're not alone. We're all just as confused."

She turned her face forward, where Kaden and Anna rode ahead of her. "Kaden, you said your mother gave you the rune. Maybe she'll know more about it."

"I suspect she would, though I have not the first notion of why she would give me the rune before—" He cut himself off. Anna turned her face to the side and rested her cheek against his back.

"Perhaps she somehow knew ye would need to use it," Aidan suggested. "She wished to take care of ye even then."

This did not seem to offer Kaden comfort, which was all Aidan had intended. He cast a worried look to Piper, who shared another soft smile.

Was he forgiven so easily? Simply because he had secured a mare for her and taught her what she needed to know about riding?

It was slow going, indeed, with Kaden lessening his pace to keep the group together. Whether he did this of his own thinking or because Anna had asked him to, Aidan could not say. But he was certain Piper would appreciate it.

As did he. Every time the lass looked the slightest bit unsteady in the saddle, it was all he could do to keep himself from reaching for her. Little good that would do, astride a mount of his own, but impulse urged him on nonetheless.

She was a strange sort. Tough, strong when she had to be, yet afraid of a simple horse. She had never slept in the out of doors before, and he'd taken note of her fretful nature as she'd settled down to sleep by the dying fire.

Every rustling in the trees had sent her eyes flying open. It had taken longer than he'd expected for her to fall asleep —yet when she had, there had been no waking her.

And for the second night in a row, he had spent part of his time watching her sleep. Asking himself what she dreamed of.

Whether there was a man in her life. Whether any man of the soft, strange time in which she lived would be worthy of her. Would a man of that time know how to manage both her strength and her fragility? Or would he be the sort to take advantage of that weakness, as so many men did even in Aidan's time?

How would he ever know? That was the worst thing of all, understanding that he would never know what she went on to do once their time together was over. She could send him no letters. The device she used to speak to people half a world away would do them no good.

Perhaps Kaden would look after her if Aidan asked him to. He decided to do just that when the time came, and the decision lightened his heart a bit.

Yet not enough that he was able to release the tightness in his chest as he watched her struggling, trying so desperately to do her best while the mare showed unfathomable patience with its inexperienced rider.

"I have to say, it's beautiful out here," she sighed. "Really, so beautiful. I don't think I've ever smelled air this clean."

"I know I haven't," Anna agreed. "I think the air in our time is better than it was, like, a century earlier thanks to less coal usage, but it's still awful compared to this. And the water is so clear!"

"I was just thinking the same thing," Piper marveled, looking down and to her left where a thin stream trickled past. "And it tastes amazing."

"Aye, but it does not come through pipes, nor does it flow at the turn of a handle," Aidan reminded her.

She stuck her tongue out at him. "Tell me you didn't enjoy that shower. I dare you to lie to me about that."

He could not lie. "Nay, I enjoyed it a great deal, to be

certain. There is something to be said for hot water when-ever one wishes for it."

"Hey! Maybe you could invent a system for it!" Piper suggested with a grin. "You would be rich and famous if you did."

"I would not know the first thing about it," he protested with a chuckle. "And I have no use for fame or riches, I can tell ye that."

"And I can tell ye he does not speak in jest," Kaden agreed. "He would live among the swine in their pen if he could."

"Thank ye, cousin," he smirked behind Kaden's back. "'Tis not quite as bad as that, ye ken. But I have never thought much of a grand life. A warm home, a bed, enough food to keep me from starving. Family, should the Lord be willing. Something I might feel proud of. That is enough for me."

"And what would make you feel proud, do you think?" There was a seriousness about Piper when she asked it. She no longer teased. Her dark eyes probed his as they rode side-by-side.

He could not avoid the question when she stared at him that way. It was unnerving, to be sure. "I could not say, not quite. Perhaps something to do with horses."

"You do seem to like them a lot."

"Aye, I do at that. I have ever found myself enjoying the time I spend with them a great deal more than I enjoy time among other men."

"Why is that?"

If she did not seem truly interested, he would not have taken the time to think the question through before giving an answer. "Perhaps 'tis because horses dinna ken what it means to hurt another. To scheme or plot or lie. I have never been able to abide by a person, man or woman, who would harm an animal. Especially a horse, when they do so much for us."

"That's very admirable."

"I dinna think of myself as admirable, though they who would beat a horse or another animal are lower than the lowest creature. I only wish to be decent." He did not much enjoy speaking of himself, especially while in the presence of the cousin who knew him so well.

Yet Kaden had quite plainly put on speed, thus lengthening the distance between himself and the riders behind him. What was the purpose of this? To have time alone to speak with his woman?

"I agree. It's just that in this time, I guessed attitudes might be different. There are groups of people in my time who work toward protecting animals of all sorts from abuse. I didn't know it was a... thing now." Piper looked ahead, a smile still playing over her face. "You would be the perfect spokesperson."

"What is that, then?"

"A spokesperson. Like, the face of the organization. The person who goes on TV or radio or online and speaks on behalf of the people in a company."

"Ye mean, appear inside the TV?" The notion filled him with unspeakable dread.

She giggled. "It isn't the way you think it is. Somebody records you with a camera and plays it on TV. You can watch yourself! You're not inside. Remember, I told you that."

"I could watch myself on the TV," he murmured, puzzled. It was all a mystery. "I believe it would already take a great deal of time to become accustomed to seeing myself in a mirror, as I did there."

Her breath caught in a strange way, her cheeks coloring before she turned her face from his. What had he said to make her behave that way?

The sun was already high in the sky, telling him they were close to the cottage. He would have known it even if clouds covered the sun, thanks to the many times he had traveled the narrow, overgrown path through the woods. Each patch of ground was familiar to him.

He understood then that Kaden was eager to reach his mother. That must have been the reason behind him riding ahead. He had suffered greatly after seeing her die, to be sure. For a moment, Aidan considered slowing further that he might give the two of them time together before being interrupted.

Which would give him time to spend talking with the lass riding beside him.

It was not to be, for he could already see the small, circular dwelling gaps in the trees. Moss-covered, nearly blending into the surroundings—which was how Isla would need it if she wished to remain safe from those who might wish to harm her simply for existing.

"Mam?" Kaden called out softly. He waited for Anna to leave the saddle before throwing a leg over and jumping to the ground, anxious to see his mam again. Aidan, however, took note of what his cousin did not.

Such as the absence of smoke coming from the hole in the thatched roof. Never had he seen her home closed-off and the fire out if she were present. At such times he would leave anything his father had sent near the door before going on his way, for there was no telling when she might return.

Sure enough, Kaden stepped from the cottage moments after he'd entered. It would not take long to search the place, as it was nothing more than a single room.

"She isn't here," he muttered, his brow lowered in concern.

17

"It doesn't mean anything bad happened to her." Anna was doing her best to calm Kaden down, the four of them sitting in the tiny little cottage which Piper had to wonder how even a single person could live in comfortably.

She tried to look at it through the eyes of a woman of that time. Especially a woman who had no choice but to hide from a world which would gladly kill her just for existing. She guessed with that in mind, a cottage in the middle of the woods that looked like something from an old children's fairytale was better than living in jail. Or hanging, or burning.

Whoever this woman was, she was a simple person with simple needs. There was nothing wrong with that. Dried herbs hung from the ceiling in bunches. They filled the air with a spicy scent which tickled the inside of her nose. It wasn't unpleasant. A small pile of blankets sat along the wall near the fire—was that the bed?—and it looked like she had just washed and dried a handful of tunics or dresses or whatever the women of those times called their clothes.

She hadn't seen a woman yet and still wondered how they dressed in these days.

Kaden's face had a stormy look to it which she recognized, and only after having known him for a couple of days. He was an intense sort of person, but she guessed he had plenty of reason to be. Especially now when he was afraid his mother was already dead, that something completely new had happened in this specific timeline and that he would never be able to prevent her from dying.

Aidan spoke up, sitting on the floor with his forearms over his bent knees. "Anna makes a good point," he murmured.

The way he spoke to his cousin then reminded her of the way he spoke to her when he was introducing her to the mare. Calm, low, no sudden moves.

He continued, "She very often goes out to collect new herbs for potions and tonics. It might be a crime to practice witchcraft, but there are young women not only of Clan MacGregor but surrounding clans, too, who visit her in hopes of her assistance."

Kaden turned to him with what looked like a grimace but was probably more like disbelief. "How would ye know that?"

"I told ye. I have been to see her many times. We speak of her life. I ask after her, I find out where she earns the few coins she uses to keep body and soul together. Did ye imagine her spending every minute of her day here, in the cottage?"

"What else was I supposed to think? She may as well

have condemned herself to death, showing herself freely among others."

Aidan's patience impressed her. He absorbed his cousin's anger but didn't give any of it back to him. "Tis not as if she dances in public with a sign hanging about her neck declaring herself to be a witch," he replied in an even tone. "She is a wise woman, skilled at keeping herself unnoticed. But tis simply not enough for ye or I to visit her once a fortnight or even less often than that. She takes care of herself."

For a second, Piper thought Kaden would explode. He certainly looked what he was about to. In fact, the darkening of his complexion and the trembling of his arms and fists give her the impression of a cartoon character about to go off like a firecracker.

Definitely not something she wanted to stick around and witness.

He didn't go off. There were no rockets, no explosions. Instead, his shoulders sagged, and a heavy sigh left him looking and sounding deflated. "I knew nothing of her," he murmured, defeated. "She was here all this time, and I told myself it was better for both of us if I kept my distance."

"But it was better for both of you! It's so dangerous, knowing a witch. Even knowing of a witch without reporting her. I can't imagine what that must be like, and how you would be persecuted just because you were born to one person to and not to another." Anna looked hopeless as she tried to comfort him, since he was not in the mood to be comforted.

"She's right." Piper hadn't planned on speaking up, but Kaden was in so much pain that she would've felt bad later if she didn't say something when she had the chance. "Sure, you wanted to help her, but you had to help yourself, too. I'm sure she wouldn't have wanted you here every day or every other day, because eventually somebody would probably follow you and know where you were going. That wouldn't be good for either of you. But more than anything, she probably just wanted you to be safe. Why else would she have sent you away? She knew what was best for you."

Aidan jumped in, his voice sounding more confident than before. "Aye, t'was simpler for me to visit when I did, for no one would think twice about my coming and going freely. Tis yourself with the attention of half the clan at all times, not myself. Ye stand out, while I do not. Perhaps that is for the best. And everyone knows my mother and my father, so they would not think it odd that I ride into the woods to visit another. However, many people know of your mother's existence and who she was; whether or not they know she is still alive is another matter which I canna speak to."

Piper nodded, glad he brought this up. "See? He could come and go as he pleased and nobody would think twice about it. If somebody noticed you, they would eventually start to ask themselves why you're riding out here and where you were going and what was so important. It was better for you to keep your distance. I'm sure if your mother were here right now, she would say the same thing."

Kaden's chuckle held no mirth, but there was no nastiness in his voice when he spoke. "You dinna know my mother," he murmured.

Piper's breath caught. Her heart ached. She didn't have to say anything else, but she felt like she should. She never really talked about before, but now was as good a time as any. "No, but I know my mother. And I know that she prefers it that I don't visit her. I want to, but she always refuses the requests."

Anna was clearly surprised by this. They had never talked about her family before. "What are you saying?" she whispered, turning away from Kaden for the first time since they had arrived.

Why was it so hard to talk about this? She was thousands of miles and hundreds of years removed from the situation, but she couldn't find it in her to form the words. "My mom... she got involved with a guy years ago. She was always with some guy or another, you know. Boyfriends. None of them were very nice. Maybe one or two were okay, but for the most part, they were the same guy in a different skin. You know what I mean? Anyway, this last one got her involved in what the judge decided was drug trafficking." She looked to the Highlanders, whose blank faces spoke of their ignorance. "That's illegal. He was getting the drugs from one place, then selling them to other people."

They both nodded, looking like they hung on her every word. Shame threatened to silence her. It was only when she reminded herself that she had done nothing wrong that she was able to keep talking.

"Of course, her boyfriend would ask her for favors, drop this off for me, pick up something for me. She just felt like she was doing him a favor, keeping him happy. Believe me, she wanted to keep the guy happy. She would've done anything for him. He had so much money. Obviously. He was a drug dealer. He used to buy her all these things, and sometimes he would try to buy things for me, too. I couldn't accept them. There was no way he was making this money legally."

She sighed, remembering the friction this caused between her and her mom. How rude she was accused of being, when she was only ever trying to do the right thing.

"I don't know if she was just too stupid to realize he was taking advantage of her, or if she deliberately let herself be taken advantage of. I mean, I hope she was ignorant of the whole thing, because she did have me to think about. But I think sometimes she forgot about me. He was good to her otherwise, and not many men had been. Still, I was just a kid, and I saw through him. She refused to. Anyway, it's the same old song. She got caught, he refused to admit she acted on his orders, and she's serving her sentence in Decatur."

Funny, how talking about something somebody else had done caused her shame. Even though she had nothing to do with it, she felt like there was something for her to be embarrassed about. Like her mother's choices had anything to do with her. If anything, had her choices anything to do with her daughter, she would have made better ones.

"She tells me she doesn't want me to come to see her because she doesn't want me to be close to that sort of thing, those kinds of people. She swears it's better for me to go on without her. Maybe she's right, but that doesn't make it any easier. Even when she says it makes her happy just to know I'm doing all right, that she doesn't need to see me so long as we can talk on the phone and she hears that I sound good. At first, I took it personally, assuming she didn't want to see me because she didn't care about me. It took a little time before I figured out that it was because she did care and was finally trying to do the right thing, even if she's sort of misguided still."

The silence that followed her little speech was profound. She could've heard a pin drop. At first, she was afraid to raise her eyes and look at any of them, wondering what they thought and why they were taking so long to say anything.

Finally, Anna joined her. She knelt beside her and put an arm around her shoulders. She then kissed her cheek, which struck Piper as very sweet. "I know it couldn't have been easy for you talk about that," she whispered. "Thank you."

Kaden's mouth opened and closed a few times before he found his voice. "I see what you mean."

Why was she afraid to look at Aidan? What did it matter what he thought of her? He was nothing, nobody. She would never see him again after this whole adventure ended.

Even so, she was embarrassed, wondering what he would think of her.

Which was why the hand he used to cover hers came as such a surprise. She hadn't expected him to do that at all. She also hadn't expected such relief, such comfort. He didn't say a word. He just held her hand for second before moving away again, but that was enough. That one gesture spoke a thousand words.

Kaden gathered himself, and when he spoke again, he sounded more assured. "What do we do now? Aidan, have ye any idea where she would have gone?"

Aidan cleared his throat. "There is a seer she often visits, a friend of hers. I only know they have a home she can easily walk to, so it canna be too difficult to make on foot."

Kaden grinned. "I know exactly who ye mean, and where she lives. Elspeth."

"Aye, that is her name."

"I remember her from when I was a lad. We might be there in under an hour." Then, Kaden frowned, scratching his head. "Tis a bit of danger, however. Traveling again with the pair of ye. Perhaps ye wish to stay behind, here at the cottage. Mam might return before Aidan, and I do."

"No offense, but I don't wanna be here alone—not that I would be alone," Anna added, looking at Piper. "But you know what I mean."

Piper nodded. "Yeah, I'm not too keen on the two of us being here without you guys. What if somebody shows up who isn't your mother? What we do then?"

Aidan went to the pile of clothing sitting by the window. "Perhaps ye might at least hide yourselves, then. Ye will not stand out quite so much if ye are wearing different clothing."

"A bonny idea," Kaden agreed.

Piper ran her hand over the rough fabric and wondered just how bonny the idea was. Then again, if it meant avoiding a noose around her neck, she would do anything.

A few minutes later, she and Anna joined the men outside. They now both wore long, shapeless dresses which came just to their ankles. They were barefoot since their shoes couldn't be explained away. "It's not like we'll be doing a lot of walking," Anna had reasoned. "A lot of people nowadays walk around barefoot."

Between that and the makeshift babushka hiding her

hair, Piper wondered how hard Aidan would laugh at her. She barely lifted her eyes to meet his as she walked out of the cottage and approached the mare.

But when she did, what she found surprised her. He was smiling, and not like he was making fun of her. "Ye look bonny," he murmured. "Truly. It suits ye."

She couldn't help but laugh. It didn't suit her at all, but he was just trying to be nice. "Thanks," she grinned, blushing a little. Or maybe that was just the sun heating her cheeks. "Even my babushka?" She patted her head.

He frowned. "What is a babushka?"

"It's a Polish word," she giggled, patting the headscarf. "My mom is Polish. Piper Kaminski. Nice to meet you."

His shoulders shook when he laughed. "Piper Kaminski. A verra interesting name."

He helped her into the saddle before climbing onto his own. For some reason, he couldn't stop looking at her. She wasn't sure if she liked it or not.

And it didn't even occur to her until they were riding away from the cottage and further from the standing stones that this was just another delay in getting home.

And for some reason, that didn't bother her too much. Not at that moment.

18

"Aye, your mam was here with me this verra day." The seer stopped stirring the pot of bubbling stew long enough to turn to them. "We had quite a bit to speak of."

"Such as what?" Kaden pressed. Never one to show patience, it was clear how he struggled to keep his voice steady.

"That is for no one's ears but mine and hers," the seer reminded him in a gentle voice. "But I did tell her she was to expect visitors from far away."

That was when her eyes fell upon the lasses, and Aidan barely controlled the impulse to stand in front of Piper. Why he felt as though he needed to protect her from a woman just as likely to face punishment for simply being who she was, he did not know. Perhaps it was a knowing glint in her eye, the wise smile which played at the corners of her lips.

Elspeth had been ancient when he was a lad, so he

could only imagine now how old she truly was. The woman's skin was thin enough to nearly be transparent, her eyes might once have been blue but were now cloudy with age. Her hair, a shockingly bright white, hung in limp strands about her weathered face.

It was a face which contained great wisdom, and he could only imagine the things she had seen without truly seeing them over her many years.

"I see the pair of ye in a shining bird." This was directed at the lasses, though Aidan could make neither heads nor tails of it.

They could, clearly.

"Are you serious?" Anna whispered, mouth hanging open.

"Och, aye. Creating music for others to enjoy. Flying through the air, above the clouds. A great deal of noise and smoke. Always running."

"Oh, this is way too bizarre," Piper whispered, clutching Aidan's arm. She trembled so.

Aidan knew enough of her world to know the seer was not far from her mark, and this was what frightened her.

"Ye have nothing to fear," he whispered, hoping he was correct.

"He is correct," the seer agreed with a smile revealing the two teeth remaining in the old woman's mouth. "I mean no harm to ye. I spoke to Isla of ye. She knows ye are on your way to her. She wished to go and fetch fresh herbs before your arrival."

Kaden let out a long sigh of relief, but Aidan's questions had not yet been answered. "Why? What do ye see her needing those herbs for? Ye make it sound as though she went out because the lasses were on their way. Why? Are they in danger?"

The old woman looked him up and down, her already creased forehead creasing more deeply. "Ye have a great deal of fear in ye," she whispered.

He barely contained a snarl. "We are not here to speak of myself. I wish to know what is to become of the lasses. Ye see danger for them?"

Piper tugged his arm now, trying to get his attention. "I don't wanna know," she whispered. "Really, Aidan. I don't wanna know."

He turned to her, confused, searching her face for answers. Now that her hair was covered and she dressed simply, she could easily have been one of the lasses from the village. He might have asked her father for the privilege of spending time with her. They might even have...

There was no use in thinking such things. "But ye dinna wish to know so ye might protect yourself?" he asked.

She shook her head. "This sort of thing freaks me out," she whispered. "Just knowing she already sees airplanes freaks me out. I mean, there's absolutely no way she could know about them. They won't be invented for another three hundred and some-odd years. She's the real deal, but I'm afraid to find out about my future."

Meanwhile, Kaden asked the seer if she could tell him exactly where he might find his mother. The old woman directed them to fields further away from the cottage where the seer herself located her herbs and flowers and barks.

"Please, should anyone ask, ye never saw us," Kaden urged her.

Elspeth waved a hand, chuckling. "Ye need not tell me. I

have seen it all, remember. I know what brings ye here, I know ye dinna intend to stay for long."

Anna crouched in front of her. "Do you see what happened before? The first time I was here?"

The woman stared at her, her expression changing from moment to moment as if she could not quite make sense of what she saw or felt. "It is dark," Elspeth admitted after some minutes, her voice taking on a dream-like sound. "There are many threads swirling about. One thread touches another, and another, but they go on their own way. All of them are joined at the top, but there is no telling where the end of each thread will go."

Piper shivered, and Aidan patted her back in a vain gesture of comfort even though the woman's words stirred concern in his breast as well.

"We had best be on our way," Kaden urged. He had a goal in mind, and nothing would keep him from that goal. Not until he found his mother would he draw an easy breath.

Aidan wondered, though he did not dare ask, precisely what Kaden planned to do once he found his mother. If he intended to return to Anna's future, what could he possibly do for Isla in this time? Warning her away from Kirk MacGregor was well and good, but the fact was he would still have to leave her without knowing what would come of her when he was gone.

Knowing it tightened Aidan's chest, made his heart heavy. His cousin might find it painful to step through the standing stone again.

"Lad." The old woman waved to him as the others took

their leave of the half-fallen stone structure which had once been a home but was now little more than ruins along the river's edge. He supposed it was safer for the seer to live this way, with less chance of anyone believing a person could live out their days with only half a roof overhead.

"Aye?" he asked. "What is it?"

"Ye have a grave choice ahead of ye," she warned. "Stay or go. I feel it in my bones. The push and pull. The moon which directs the tides, pulling the water back toward itself. Will ye follow the pull of the moon, I wonder?"

The moon? He would have openly scoffed were it not for wishing to avoid insulting the old woman.

Then, the wistfulness left her. The woman's face hardened like stone. "T'was not for the lasses Isla searched for her herbs," she said in a flat voice. "T'was for yourself."

He gaped at her. "Myself? For me?"

"Aye. Ye shall be in need of her ministrations before the sun rises twice more. Take heed." She turned away then, giving her attention to the stew over the fire.

He would need Isla's help. Why?

It was then that Piper's hesitation came to mind. She had not wished to know. It was easier not to know. Better, too. He understood now. It was better if the woman did not tell him why. Less than two days' time. That was all he needed to know.

"Aidan? You coming?" Piper asked from outside. One look through the doorway told him she had managed to mount the mare without his assistance. A rush of pride nearly knocked him off his feet. A fine lass, brave and strong.

"Aye," he replied. "I am."

And he was. And he would not have told her for anything in the world what Elspeth had just shared. Better to see her smile, to note the prideful upward tilt of her chin as he joined her. She had every right to be proud of herself.

"What do you think?" she asked, preening a bit. "I've come a long way in a few hours, haven't I?"

"Aye, ye have at that," he agreed as he settled into the saddle. "Ye might be a fine horsewoman yet."

"I don't have much of a need for that in the middle of Chicago," she reminded him. "But you never know. Maybe one day I'll have horses of my own. And I'll remember—"

Her voice faltered, her shoulders sank. The prideful tilt of her chin was no more. She let out a long breath and did not finish speaking her thought.

She did not need to. He knew well what she had been about to say and had no desire to hear it.

They rode in silence then, which was for the best. Aidan needed every bit of concentration he could muster, ever watchful of any who might be riding nearby. The woods were thinner here, with greater gaps in the trees which allowed for more sunlight and more visibility.

The lasses might have appeared to be young women from the time, but anyone who might engage them in conversation would know in an instant there was something wrong. Better to be aware of the possibility, then, rather than being surprised.

For all the seer's insistence that the field in which she gathered her herbs was nearby, Aidan could not help but wonder just how long they would ride. The sun was now beginning its downward journey through the sky, and he had begun to think Isla had moved on and they would never find her when the trees thinned and opened upon a field of wild growing herbs and flowers. Their scent filled the air, carried to the riders on the breeze. Sweet and spicy and musky, all together.

And there she was. Aidan's heart lightened at the sight of long, gray-streaked hair blowing in the breeze. She worked with her back to them, bending and gathering, plucking stems and dropping them into a basket over one arm.

They dismounted, with Kaden running across the field to meet his mother. Anna wept, hands over her mouth, while Piper sniffled and ran a hand beneath both eyes as though to catch her tears.

She had a soft heart, one befitting a woman.

This did not explain, then, why Aidan found himself a bit choked up at the sight of mother and son reunited. Kaden threw his arms around her, lifting her from her feet, all but crushing the woman in his joy.

It seemed fitting for Aidan to slide an arm around Piper's shoulders then. He reasoned that the lass should not weep silently, alone, with no one to comfort her or to silently express how moved they were as well.

The gratitude with which she looked up at him all but took his breath away. Were she any other lass, he might have taken her chin in one hand and bent to kiss her upturned mouth.

Even then, knowing well that it would be a mistake, the impulse tugged at him. Just one kiss. It would disturb nothing. He only wished to kiss her once, to carry the memory of her in his heart always. This strange, difficult, warm and caring woman.

He could not.

Yet he kept her by his side, his arm around her, watching as mother and son rejoiced to be together again.

19

———

"This all so strange," Kaden observed as they stood together alongside the horses. "I have introduced ye before, and yet I need to do it again. Mam, this is Anna."

Anna had barely stopped sobbing and let out a hitching little gasp as she took a woman's hand. "It is so wonderful to see you," she managed to choke out.

It was beyond trippy, and Piper hadn't even met the woman before. Anna had watched her die and worn her blood on her clothes.

"'Tis a blessing to meet ye, my dear." Isla patted her hand before turning to Aidan. "And yourself. It has been long enough since last I saw ye, and that is a fact."

Aidan chuckled. "I was riding with the men," he told her. "To Fraser land. Were it not for that, I would have seen ye."

"Och, men and your important plans." She waved a dismissive hand, chuckling. "And who is this, then?"

Aidan turned to her, his jaw working that he was trying to figure out exactly what to say.

When he didn't speak right away, she turned to Isla. "I am Piper," she explained. "It's very nice to meet you."

"Piper, is it?" Isla nodded, her lips pursed. "An interesting name. Is that your given name?"

Piper blushed. She never imagined being in the hot seat, answering questions about herself or her mother's choice in names. "Yes, it is."

"I like it," the woman decided with a firm nod.

Kaden couldn't seem to stop touching her, stroking her hair or rubbing her shoulder like he needed to remind himself that she was alive and well and standing next to him. Piper couldn't help but wonder if he would ever let her go again. "I cannot believe I have ye back," he murmured.

"I dinna ken what ye mean. I have gone nowhere. What reason would ye have to get me back at all? Why do ye make it seem as though ye were surprised to find me?"

It was funny. Mothers through the centuries had not lost their ability to look at their child in just such a way that made it impossible to tell a lie. That was how the much smaller, gray-haired, trouser-wearing woman looked up at her hulking, powerful son just then.

And he practically melted into a puddle. He shifted from one foot to the other, uncomfortable. Piper could understand why. How did a person tell their mother that they had watched them die?

It was Aidan who spoke up. "The hour grows late. Perhaps we ought to set out for the cottage now, before darkness falls. All can be explained then."

Kaden wore the look of a man who had just been spared execution. Piper thought he might throw his arms around Aidan in relief. Instead, he cleared his throat, nodding decisively. "Aye, that would be wise."

Except there was a problem. Isla didn't have a horse with her. "I dinna need to ride," she insisted.

"Nay, ye shall ride. I will not have ye walking through the dark, as it will take longer to reach the cottage on foot and will surely be darker by then." Kaden looked to Piper, then to the mare whose reins she held.

If Isla rode the mare, what would she do?

"Oh," she breathed. The only options were to either ride behind Isla or behind…

"Ye need not fret," Aidan assured her once he read the situation for what it was. "I shall not bite ye or throw ye from the saddle."

She rolled her eyes even though he was clearly joking. "That's what I call a glowing endorsement." But there was no other choice to be made. She would have to ride with him the way Anna rode with Kaden.

Of course, it wouldn't be the same way. She wouldn't lean against him way Anna leaned against her man. She wouldn't rest her cheek on his back.

But she would have to hold onto his waist. She would have to be that close to him.

Which was probably why her pulse raced. Why her hands shook as Aidan reached down for her. Kaden helped, lifting her up and waiting until she was settled behind Aidan before mounting his horse. Anna made it look so easy when she climbed up behind him.

"Are ye comfortable?" Aidan asked, turning his face slightly so he could see her from the corner of his eye.

Was she comfortable? No, not in any way, shape or form. Not physically, not emotionally. It did not thrill her, having to put her arms around his waist. She didn't enjoy being this close to him. She didn't like feeling his strong body in her arms, his thighs against her thighs. It was miserable.

Maybe if she kept telling herself this, she would believe it. Maybe it would be true.

Because truthfully, at that very minute, she couldn't have enjoyed herself more. It was too much of a thrill, and that was dangerous. "I'm okay," she managed to choke out.

"Your arms are trembling, which is why I asked."

"This horse is much bigger than the mare," she pointed out. That definitely wasn't a lie, even if it was the reason she was trembling.

"Worry not. We shall ride swiftly and return to the cottage before the sun sets."

That did absolutely nothing to ease the frenzy her thoughts were in, but she smiled anyway and tried to reassure him as best she could.

This was so unfortunate.

He was just a man. That was all. There were plenty of men in the world. The sixteen hundreds didn't have a corner on the market for strong, virile men. Rugged men who lived their lives outside, whose skin was always tanned by the sun. Whose thighs were roughly the size of tree trunks and looked like they could crack walnuts. Aidan wasn't the only one.

But he was the only one who she'd ever responded to

this way. She almost didn't know what to do with herself and was glad he couldn't see the furious flushing of her cheeks every time their bodies collided—which was a lot, no matter how she tried otherwise if only for the sake of modesty.

And to think. She was about to return to a time when he would be long dead.

Her heart clenched at the thought. Her arms tightened around him, like she could hold him with her if she tried hard enough. He would be long gone, dead for hundreds of years. But he was alive with her now, alive and real and strong. Her brain couldn't seem to catch up to reality, especially when the physical evidence was right here in front of her. Evidence of him being alive and well and strong and healthy.

Maybe she shouldn't have come.

The thought took her by surprise, as it wasn't a conscious thought. More like something that had occurred to her as it bubbled up from her subconscious. If she hadn't come, she would've been sad to say goodbye to someone who had made her last twelve hours more interesting than any twelve hours she'd ever spent.

Sure, she probably would've gone have crazy wondering and worrying about Anna. That might have been easier than growing closer to the man she was now pressed against. It would've been easier than caring about him.

And she definitely wouldn't have wished that he had stayed with her.

That was the real problem. She understood then, in that very moment as she sat behind him in the saddle. She wanted him to come with her. Why should he want to stay behind in this world? There was nothing for him here.

"Why did ye sigh?" he asked.

They rode in the back of the line, with Isla riding beside Kaden. He wanted it that way. He wouldn't let the woman out of his sight if he could help it. This gave them a little bit of privacy, though Aidan kept his voice low just in case.

She already knew why he did certain things without having to ask. That wasn't good.

"Did I sigh?" she asked, trying to be casual.

"Ye did, loud enough for me to hear. Is there something troubling ye?"

Why did he have to be so nice? Why did he have to care? If he had gone along with being a jerk, like one of the men she had known when she was a kid whose her mom tied herself up with one loser after another, it would've been one thing.

But no, he had to be nice and concerned and caring. He had to take the time to show her how to ride a horse and how to not be afraid. What a creep.

"I don't quite know," she admitted. "I guess it makes me sad to think of leaving here." *You. Leaving you. And it terrifies me and makes me sadder than I've been in a long time.*

"Ye make it sound as if that is a bad thing."

"Well it isn't exactly a good thing," she reminded him, miserable. "I mean, it's not like a friend moving away, where I can still call them or send a text message when we're both watching the same show at the same time."

"Ye have lost me."

She nudged him. "No, I haven't. You know what I mean. Stop trying to pretend that I'm speaking another language.

I guess you'll miss Kaden, too, and it's not like you can ride a couple of hours to where he'll be or send him a message or something. You get it?"

He grunted, facing straight ahead. "Aye. I ken what ye mean all too well. Perhaps 'tis simpler for me to pretend I dinna."

"So you get it?"

"Of course I do." Then, he snorted. "I must say it surprises me to hear ye use the word friend."

"Is that such a surprise?" She laughed in spite of herself. "I don't do the sort of things I've done for you for just anybody, you know. Introducing you to twenty-first-century technology. Showing you how to use the shower, though I have to admit that was just as much for my benefit as it was for yours."

He laughed loudly enough that Isla turned in surprise. She flashed a fond smile before turning her attention to her son again.

"Ye make a fair point," Aidan admitted. "And it pains me as well, lass. Dinna think it doesn't. I dislike the notion of sending ye back to that world. There are so many dangers there."

"There are dangers here, too! Like infection, for one thing. You live in a time when a person can die from a scratch they didn't clean properly."

"Ye mean to tell me I am supposed to clean my skin when 'tis scratched?"

"Oh, you gotta be kidding me."

He chuckled, the sound rumbling inside him close to her ear. "Aye, lassie. I am kidding ye."

She clenched her hands into one large fist and jammed

it against his abdomen, not hard, but enough to get her point across. "Here I am, trying to be thoughtful and God forbid care about you a little bit, and you're making a joke out of it."

"Pardon me," he replied, still chuckling a little bit. "What else do I need to know, then? How else do ye wish to protect me from this dangerous world?"

"No. Forget it. You think you're so smart, so you're not going to listen to anything. Maybe you don't deserve my help."

Kaden turned to them. "With the pair of ye chattering on so, 'tis a wonder to me we have not attracted attention from men riding even at a distance."

She stuck her tongue out, knowing he couldn't possibly see her with Aidan between them. He wasn't the sort of guy she would've stuck her tongue out to if there was a chance of him seeing it. She wasn't crazy.

That seemed to be enough to placate Aidan, who was also smart enough not to get on his cousin's bad side. Even so, she whispered, "I just don't want to see you die for some stupid reason that could've been avoided. That's all."

"Aye, as I would like to see ye not die because ye stepped foot into the road and was struck by one of those cars."

"That's what traffic lights are for. Remember? Red means stop?"

"Dinna tell me 'tis not possible to be struck. I saw it on the TV when ye slept."

"Oh, so he thinks he knows all about the twenty-first century just because he watched a few hours of TV."

"And she thinks she knows all about my time simply because she has spent a handful of hours here."

She scoffed. "That's where you're wrong, buddy. I learned about times like this in school. And you all had a pretty high mortality rate for all kinds of stupid reasons."

"I dinna appreciate being called stupid."

"I wasn't calling you stupid. I was calling the time you live in stupid." This was devolving beautifully. She knew she should take it back and apologize, but not when he insisted there was something wrong in the time she had come from.

At least she wasn't half as turned on as she was earlier. That was a relief. Now, she wanted to throw him out of the saddle and kick him if he tried to get back up into it.

Why couldn't she say what she really felt? That she was worried for him. She would always worry about him and wonder what had become of him. That she would make it her life's mission to learn more about her family if only because there would be a chance of learning about him.

Then again, there would be the chance of learning that he had married some girl and had children and a good life. Not that there was anything wrong with that, but still. It would hardly make her happy.

It would make her just about as happy as she was then, mad at herself for not having the courage to tell him why she was really upset. To make things right while there was still a chance.

20

———

The familiar cottage was even more familiar thanks to the warm light of the fire which Isla stirred to life. Shadows played along the walls, and the scent of so many fresh herbs and plants was soothing. It brought to mind many years spent sitting on that very floor, both as a lad and as a man.

It was little wonder that his cousin had never known Aidan considered this a second home. Not that his own home was not a fine place—indeed, while it may not have been grand, it had always been filled with love.

Yet there had ever been something which drew him to Isla's cottage. Perhaps the sense of being understood without the need to say a word. She knew him better than he knew himself at times.

Which he could only imagine was the reason why she insisted on looking at him again and again, and always with a knowing smile. Her gaze would on occasion brush over Piper before returning to him, and that smile would grow.

He wished she wouldn't, most fervently so. There was

nothing to be done about their differences. They could not seem to spend more than a few minutes together without arguing. And how she had stiffened when riding behind him, as if the act brought her considerable pain.

It seemed that even a skilled witch could not be aware of everything. He resolved to set her straight at the first opportunity.

Isla sat at her table, with Kaden across from her and the rest of them seated on the floor. She looked over the group, studying each of them in turn. "What ye have told me is strange and wondrous indeed," she surmised in her usual quiet voice.

"Aye, 'tis that," Kaden agreed. "Ye have no idea how it pained me—"

She hushed him, a finger to her lips. "My son. Do ye ken why I believe all ye have said? Because what ye described is precisely what I would do as your mam. I would do it again now if need be. Stepping in front of a bolt is nothing compared to the lengths a mother would go to for her child. Truly, I would do that and more if it meant sparing ye."

Why this made Aidan look to Piper, he could not say. The downward turn of her mouth told him that she had taken Isla's words just as he had. It made her think of her own mother.

The rune sat in the center of the table, dark and cold as if its power slumbered while it was not close to the standing stone. "Do ye know why ye would have given this to me in your final moments?" Kaden asked.

"I do," she whispered. "Tis a rune passed down from my

grandmother's grandmother, and perhaps before that. It holds great power."

"We know that," Anna agreed with a shaky laugh.

"Aye, that we do," Aidan added. "For were it not for that rune and for Kaden dropping it, I would never have stumbled into the future."

"Did ye stumble, though? Truly?" Her brows lifted as she turned her gaze upon him. "Or was it meant to come to pass?"

A chill ran down his spine when their eyes met. He did not like it, not at all. The way she seemed to look through him. While feeling as though she understood his deepest thoughts and wishes was pleasant and comforting at times, it could chill him to the bone at others.

As it did then. He would rather not have her share his thoughts and suspicions with the rest of the group.

Try as he might, he could not sound amused when he laughed. "What would ye call it, then?" he asked. Though he would not look her way, he felt Piper staring at him.

"I would say there is a reason why both my son and my son's cousin happened to locate the rune. Tell me, were ye the first man to stand guard at the henge after Kaden used the rune to escape to the future?"

"Nay, there were many others before me. Hours had passed by then."

"Yet none of them found the rune lying on the ground. It was ye who found it, ye who used it though ye were unaware of its power. Is that not so?"

He now understood what she was trying to say. "Aye, 'tis so."

"Ye dinna find it strange that it happened to be yourself? And not one who would use the rune and somehow lose it entirely?" She nodded to Piper. "And ye happened to come through the stone at the very moment this lass was present? A lass who already knew the lass who found my son in this time? Does it not seem all very strange and far too great a coincidence?"

Piper leaned forward. "Are you trying to say it was fate? That there's something out there pulling us all together? Is that what you mean?"

Isla smiled with a warmth and fondness which surprised Aidan. They had only just met, yet she seemed to take a liking to the newcomer. "Fate? Perhaps. Perhaps there has been a plan all along, for all four of ye. Perhaps it was meant to be, my death in the other time ye described."

"Dinna say that," Kaden warned with a catch in his throat.

"My son, were it not for my death then, ye would not have come into possession of the rune. Dinna ye ken? Ye might have been able to escape this time with the help of the marking on Anna's arm. But Aidan would never have gone through, and he would never have met this lass. That means a great deal."

If there was one impulse Aidan had always struggled to break himself of, it was his tendency to laugh when deeply uncomfortable. It had caused him no small amount of grief over time.

Much like the grief it cost him then when laughter bubbled up in his chest and escaped his open mouth.

Piper glared at him, obviously hurt by his reaction. He stammered, silently cursing his foolishness. "I dinna mean to offend ye, lass," he stammered, more uncomfortable than ever. This did little to satisfy her if the way she turned from him meant anything.

Isla appeared sympathetic. "There are ever events taking place in our lives, the importance of which we dinna see until far later. There are times, however, when we see the importance much sooner. Now, perhaps Anna was meant to come to Scotland, to visit the verra place where the henge exists. Your festival, as ye call it, might have taken place anywhere in the world. But it took place here. That means a so much. All of this, everything which has taken place, has taken place for a reason. For myself, it gives me great comfort to know that nothing I have ever suffered or ever struggled against has been in vain. T'was all meant to serve a higher purpose."

They sat in silence for a long time, all of them trying to understand what the witch explained. All the while, as her words wove themselves around those who sat listening intently, did she work with a mortar and pestle to grind combinations of barks and plants, leaves and flowers.

He understood that some of this might have been for him, and again his thoughts turned to Piper. The seer had warned him it would be before the sun rose a second time when he would need the use of what Isla now prepared.

He looked to her, and she watched him from beneath lowered brows. He dipped his chin just once, telling her without words that he knew. She did the same, then turned her gaze back to her work.

Judging by the amount she made, whatever was coming to him would be grave, indeed. Now he wished he had asked the seer what awaited him, that he could prepare himself.

Strange, but the only thing which brought him a measure of relief was knowing that he would send Piper back to her own time in the morning, just as soon as they made it to the henge. She need not be there when injury befell him.

"How does the rune work, exactly?" Piper asked after a spell. "Am I right when I assume that because Kaden and Aidan came back to this time, the versions of themselves who were here before that moment ceased to be?"

Isla nodded, her hands working the ground herbs. "That is so. The same thing might not exist at the same time. If ye were to return to your time now, ye would not see yourself. Ye would be yourself."

"And when we leave, then?" Kaden asked, a note of hope in his voice. As if he need not blame himself for leaving his mother alone. "What will happen then? Will I be here then?"

"I am afraid not, my son. Ye will be gone, and all will wonder what happened to ye. That is how the rune's power works. We will remember ye, of course, and people will question where ye went, what befell ye. Of course, none of them will come close to understanding the truth of it, but that is for the best. They would certainly never accept it."

"Are you really a witch?" Piper asked. "Or is it just that you know how to use nature to help other people? Is it just that your family was in possession of that rune for all these generations, and it's the rune that has power?"

Kaden winced, as did Anna. Perhaps they felt Isla might take this to heart, as if Piper questioned the woman's abilities and found her lacking.

It was only Aidan and Isla herself who seemed to

understand the nature of the question. "I have asked myself that verra thing many times," she admitted. "I could not say with all certainty. I protect the rune, just as I use the knowledge my mother and grandmother passed on to me when I was just a lass of your age and younger. That has always been a way for us, and men have never understood."

Piper snorted. "I wish I could say that's changed over the centuries, but..."

Anna chuckled along with her. "You might not be burned at stake in our time, but you probably wouldn't be taken seriously by a lot of people."

"Perhaps that is simply how it is meant to be." None of this seemed to bother her much, and indeed she seemed eager to speak of other things. "Ye intend to ride to the henge tomorrow, then?"

"Aye, we do." Kaden reached across the table, covering his mother's hands with his own. He engulfed her, though Aidan had the sense that were the woman to decide to free herself, she could easily do so. There was a core of iron in her center. "I dinna wish to leave ye. Perhaps ye could come with us."

"What is meant to be, will be." She shook Kaden's hands off then—gently, but with determination—and continued in her work.

Aidan cleared his throat. "I will see to the horses," he started as he rose from the floor. "And we might have a small fire out there to warm ourselves."

"I do wish there were space indoors for all of ye," Isla murmured.

"Fret not," Kaden assured her. He tried to sound lighthearted, but his attempt fell far short of its mark. He was deeply unhappy, wishing his mother would follow. He did not want to leave her, and naturally, Aidan could understand this.

It was his choice to join Anna in the future. There was no need to go—there did not seem to be the same danger as there had been before his first journey to that future world. He might remain, no longer hunted, no longer in jeopardy.

Yet he would not, for it would mean sending his love without him. That was his choice to make, but he could not expect the rest of them to make the choices he wished for them as a result. He could not both follow his love and bid his mother give up her life and all she'd ever known simply to please and comfort him.

He could not have his way in all things.

None of them could.

21

The last thing Piper felt like seeing as she stirred to wakefulness in the middle of the night was the sight of Kaden and Anna huddled together on the other side of the dying fire.

She rolled her eyes, turning over so her back was to them. Did they have a shred of self-awareness? Had it ever occurred to them that not everybody would want to watch them sleeping side-by-side, curled up together, sharing the other's warmth?

She sounded like a bitter old woman, and she knew it. Just like she knew she was jealous.

She couldn't help it. Anna found her love. Sure, they had faced obstacles together, but they overcame them. And he had chosen her, which said more about him than anything else could. He chose a life he knew nothing about because he couldn't imagine living without her.

How was she supposed not to be jealous of that? How was she supposed to keep herself from longing for something she would never have?

The hard ground under her and the chill in the air probably weren't making things much better. She was miserable because of her surroundings, nothing more. None of this had anything to do with Anna in particular, or with Kaden.

Or with Aidan.

She let out a shuddering sigh at the thought of him. Where was he? Probably sleeping closer to the cottage, feeling like he ought to guard Isla while they were there. That was his way.

It was only because she had never met decent men before this that she felt so strangely connected to him. She knew it, and reminded herself so many times. Maybe if she said it enough, it would be true.

She should never have come here.

The sound of nearby footsteps stopped her heart. She froze, wondering if she ought to pretend to be asleep or maybe jump up and run. But again, where would she run to in the dark?

It was only Aidan. That made twice that he had come out of nowhere and surprised her.

And she surprised him in return when she sat up. He jumped back a little, startled. "I thought ye were asleep," he whispered, careful not to wake the others.

"I thought you were, too. Where were you?"

He grimaced, shaking his head. "Does not occur to ye that a man might need a moment's privacy in the middle of the night?"

She blushed and turned her face away. "Right. Sorry."

"And yourself? Why are ye not sleeping? I would think

that after so much riding today, ye would be near the point of exhaustion."

Funny how just the mention of the riding they had done made her thighs ache and her butt tingle, and not in a pleasant way. She could barely walk by the time they'd arrived at the cottage after finding Isla. "I just woke up, is all. I was gonna try to go back to sleep."

"Oh, forgive me for disturbing ye, then. Take your rest while ye can."

The funny thing was, she didn't want to now. She had him to herself for little while, probably the last time she ever would.

With that in mind, the thought of sleeping struck her as a waste of time. "What will you tell everybody when they ask what happened to Kaden?"

He stirred the dying fire to new life, silent for a long time. The light played off his twitching jaw, signaling his uncertainty and his strain. "I canna say. I suppose I shall pretend not to know."

"I guess you're going to have to pretend not to know a lot of things," she observed, watching him closely. Her heart ached for him. He was so troubled, and there was nothing she could do about it but watch him fall deeper and deeper into a dark place.

"Aye, I suppose I will," he finally sighed.

He wouldn't look at her. Maybe that was what kept her from lying back down the way she knew she should. Why she got to her knees and crawled over to where he crouched.

He tensed, bringing to mind a skittish animal.

When she spoke, it was in a soothing tone just like she

had used with the mare. Like he had used with her when she was getting over her fright. "I'm sorry."

He scoffed, still staring into the fire. "Sorry? For what do ye have to be sorry, lass?"

"For leaving you here, holding the bag for us. Lying, telling people you don't know what happened to Kaden. Pretending you don't know about the future even though if I were you, I would want to tell everybody. But you can't, it would be way too dangerous for you. I'm sorry for that, too. And I'm sorry I got mad at you earlier. Sometimes, when I don't know how to say what I really wanna say, it makes me mad."

His body relaxed in stages, the tension draining from his shoulders, his arms and his back until he seemed much more at ease that he had been before. "Did I tell ye there was once a time when I wished to know the future? Not far into the future, not your future, but my own? I once asked Kaden's mother to read tea leaves for me. A daft notion, to be sure, but I was a young man. I wanted to know what would become of me."

"What did she see?"

He took a deep breath before speaking. His brows drew together over the bridge of his nose as a look of concentration swept over his face. "She told me I would meet a woman from far away. That this woman would come a great distance. That was all. At least, all that I can remember of it. I was verra disappointed, as ye can imagine. It was not clear enough for me, with the little patience afforded a lad."

Meanwhile, Piper could barely breathe. A woman from

far away? Did that distance have to be in miles? Could it have been years?

The softening of his expression when he turned to her told her she wasn't alone in asking these questions. "And there are other things I know, nothing specific but enough to weigh on my heart tonight. And tomorrow ye will leave, and I canna follow. That also weighs heavily on me—far heavier than ye might appreciate."

She was melting. Turning into a puddle of mush thanks to the light in his eyes, just like the light she had seen that morning. A light in the darkness that shouldn't have been there, a light which seemed to reach out to her and hold her attention. Light which wrapped itself around her and drew her in, sort of like the light that came from the rune before they had entered the past.

"You can come with us," she whispered. Then, throwing her pride aside, she added, "I wish you would. I really do."

"Piper—"

"Wait, please. Hear me out. I know there's a lot of differences between this time and my time, but I'm there. I would be there for you. We could figure it out together."

Oh, God, was she saying these things? How stupid would they sound to him? There he was, a man of great pride, she was practically begging him to turn his back on everything he had ever known in favor of following her to a place that obviously scared him senseless.

"I have no doubt," he murmured, a thin smile tugging at the corners of his mouth. He looked younger when he smiled, and more handsome than ever. God, she could get lost in his eyes, especially when he smiled. She couldn't even stand to look at him any longer for fear that she would throw herself into his arms and firmly cement her place as the stupidest woman in the world.

Yes, she was stupid. If she cared anything about him, she wouldn't make his decision more difficult by trying to twist him up into doing what she wanted him to do. That wasn't fair. She needed to think about him, too, and that meant not forcing him into something that would make him unhappy.

Even if it meant she could make him happy. But she couldn't guarantee that, could she? They were too different. He would expect her to be the sort of woman who grew up in that time; subservient, always listening to his opinion and taking it as law. Unable to have a say in her own life.

She already watched a woman destroy herself that way. She wasn't about to make the same mistakes her mother had made.

"It was just an idea," she whispered, moving away again as her heart threatened to tighten hard enough to kill her. It was already hard to breathe, and getting harder all the time. What she really wanted to do was cry, but she wouldn't dare. Not in front of him.

"Please, dinna—" he murmured.

She cut him off before he could say anything he might regret. "No, it's okay. Really. I wasn't thinking. And I am tired. I'm not in my right mind. Forget I said anything." She hoped he didn't see the tears filling her eyes as she crawled back to her makeshift bed and placed her head on the saddle, wrapping her arms around herself to ward off the chill.

More rustling, and this time it was his turn to come to her. He knelt beside her, reaching down to brush the hair away from her forehead. She tried to turn her face away, to avoid him, but he wouldn't take the hint. "It would be fine if ye would just once allow a man to speak before ye decide to turn away from him," he murmured.

"You don't need to say anything. I'm just trying to make it easier for you. Don't feel like there's anything you have to say, because there isn't. I spoke before I thought, big surprise. I've been doing that my entire life."

"But I wish to speak. Ye might at least give me the chance to say what is on my mind."

"Fine. What do you have to say?" He couldn't possibly have any idea how much pain this was causing her. It was one thing to speak out of turn, but another to have it rubbed in her face that she made a huge mistake in hoping he would decide to join her. It would be a lot easier if he would leave her alone.

Then again, nothing about this had been easy, so why would she expect this to be?

"I wish to tell ye that I have a life here. I have friends here. My family is here. Once Kaden has gone, Isla will have no one but myself and my father, and my father canna be seen riding to her cottage. He will surely attract attention. So ye see? How am I to turn my back on all of them?"

Sure. That meant she wasn't enough to make up for all of that, the way Anna was enough to make up for everything Kaden was leaving behind.

The worst part was, she respected him for it. She couldn't even hold it against him. What sort of hypocrite would that make her? He was a good guy behaving the way could guys behaved.

She swallowed over the lump in her throat and

managed to nod. "I get it. I really do. You don't have to explain it to me."

"Then why do I feel as though I do? Perhaps I wish for ye to understand. Perhaps I want to at least be able to tell myself when ye are gone that I said what needed saying. There will be no making up for what we did do not say to each other once ye step through the stone."

He brushed her hair back again, this time letting his fingers linger on her cheek. She didn't push him away. If anything, she wished he would do more.

She pushed herself up on her elbow, then rested her weight on her palm as she sat facing him. "I can't stay here," she whispered, eyes darting back and forth over his face. She had to memorize him. She couldn't forget a single thing, not the curve of his jaw or the way the light played over the planes of his cheeks, the line of his shoulders.

"I know that. It does not need to be said."

"Perhaps I wish for you to understand," she whispered in an echo of what he'd just said.

It happened so suddenly, he took her breath away. One second it was just the two of them facing each other in the light from the fire, and the next she was in his arms, and he was holding her close to him, and they were kissing each other like it was last thing they would ever do.

Tears rolled down her cheeks, her arms wrapping around his neck and squeezing hard enough to hurt because he was hers, just for now, and she had to make the most of it.

He kissed her hard enough to hurt, her lips throbbing. But she didn't stop him. In fact, she kissed him harder, wishing it didn't have to be the first and last time.

It was magic, it was exhilarating, and she was too dizzy to think straight, but that didn't matter because there was only one truth she cared about and that was the truth of him. It was just the two of them then, the two of them in their own world.

For that moment, it didn't matter which time either of them came from or whether they could stay together.

They were together at that moment, and that was enough.

Until it wasn't.

Until the hands which ran up and down her back went still.

Until his lips didn't press against hers with the same urgency.

She leaned away, breaking the last bit of magic between them. She felt it dissolve like cotton candy under a drop of water. It melted away. All that was left was the aching in her lips and the rise and fall of her chest as she fought to control her breathing.

That, and the continuing pain in her chest.

"Ye had best sleep," he grunted, looking away from her. His hands were clenched in tight fists, so tight his knuckles stood out bone white beneath his tanned skin. Whether it was anger or frustration or simply the need to control himself, she didn't know and wouldn't dare ask. Some things didn't need to be said.

She lowered herself to the blanket without saying a word and curled up in a protective ball before closing her eyes.

And she pretended not to notice when Aidan spread a blanket over her.

22

The most troubling part of having kissed her was the way the memory refused to leave him. It colored his feelings toward her, feelings which had already been dangerously warm and protective before those mad moments by the fire.

Many a lass had been kissed by him, but never had he felt this way about them afterward. If anything, once the mad rush of passion passed, he was left feeling rather disenchanted by the entire affair. More times than not he had wished it had never happened, because lasses had the tendency to think more of such things than a man did.

Nothing could have been further from the truth at this verra moment. Now, he understood why those young women had wished to attach themselves to him. Now he understood why they had sought him out whenever they happened to be in the same company.

He could not keep his eyes from her that morning, and he could not stop the rush of memory when she climbed into the saddle behind him and wrapped her arms around his waist.

For just a moment, she had been his.

He had been a fool for giving in to what his heart and his body had so needed at that moment.

Yet if he had he never kissed her, if he had never found a way to tell her without words what she had come to mean to him, he would have cursed himself for the remainder of his life for that lost opportunity.

Now, it would be more difficult than ever to let her go, but it was never going to be easy. At least now she might remember him. She might know as the years went on that somewhere in the past, a man had loved her. She might take comfort in knowing that he would never forget her until his dying day.

For even when she was infuriating him, he loved her. Even when she turned her back on him and forced him to follow her, to make her listen to him when she did not wish to do so, he loved her. He would never debase himself or make himself out to be a fool if it were not for love.

He would never force her to stay with him, because he loved her enough to know this was not her time. She would be branded a witch, for certain, and he would be the worst type of fool to tell himself otherwise.

Just as he would have been a fool to believe he could make sense of the time in which she lived.

He followed Kaden away from the cottage, with Isla riding the gray mare as she had from returning from her herb gathering. She had insisted on coming along with them, wishing to be present that her son might say his final goodbye to her. No amount of protestation from either of them was enough to change her mind.

Kaden seemed eager to return to Anna's time, which baffled Aidan. How could anyone wish to be there? How could anyone look forward to life in a world not meant for them?

This question plagued him throughout the first half of their ride, as the sun climbed higher in the sky and they drew closer to their destination. After several hours they dismounted to water the horses and stretch their legs, and this was when Aidan took the chance of pulling Kaden aside.

"What is it?" Kaden asked, concerned. "Is there trouble?"

Aidan found himself at a loss for words. He shook his head. "I wished to say goodbye," he lied. "As there might be time once we arrive at the henge."

Kaden smiled, clasping arms with his cousin. "Verra well. Take care of yourself. Do not allow Kirk to bedevil your father if ye can manage it."

"Ye dinna need to tell me," Aidan assured him. "And yourself. Please, if ye would, look after..."

Kaden sighed. "Aye, I had wondered if ye would speak of what happened last night."

"What do ye mean?"

He chuckled. "Did ye believe ye were silent? That no one would hear ye speaking to each other? Ye didna take pains to whisper."

Aidan bristled under the knowledge that they'd been overheard. That his cousin knew what a fool he'd been. But again, Kaden was a fool when it came to Anna. Perhaps he would understand.

The sympathy in his eyes told Aidan he did, in fact, understand. "I am sorry for ye both, I truly am. This is terribly difficult. Perhaps that is the way things were meant to be all along."

"Ye sound like your mam," Aidan grumbled. That was not what he needed to hear then, that there was a power at work in their lives. He had never been one to believe in such things. Even if he had once asked Isla to look into his future.

That was different.

Kaden shrugged good-naturedly, taking no offense. "Perhaps she speaks the truth. Ye must admit, it seems strange no one took notice of the rune before ye did. And that Piper happened to be there just when ye came through."

"I dinna believe there is a force guiding my life," Aidan argued. "Nor do I wish for there to be."

"Nor do I, but no amount of wishing it were otherwise changes anything. I might wish all I want to be the only thing guiding my life, yet that does not change anything."

He took Aidan by the shoulders, looking him straight in the eye. "Dinna turn your back on that which might bring ye great joy simply because ye are too stubborn to accept it. Ye will not get another chance to take what it is ye want. I ask ye to keep this in mind as we ride."

He turned away before Aidan had a chance to argue, bending to take several palms full of water into his mouth before returning to Anna. It had once struck Aidan as rather soft of his cousin, the way his face lit up whenever he was in her presence.

Now, he thought he understood, little good though it did him.

Piper would not speak to him as they resumed their ride. He was very glad of this, for he would not have known what to say if she tried. It seemed there was much to be said, but he had not the words to explain himself.

After all, he had already tried, and look where he had gotten them. They had ended things no closer to an understanding then they had begun. If anything, their kiss had only added to the confusion.

All he could do as they rode away the hours was reflect on those heart-racing moments, holding them in his memory along with the sweet presence of her body behind his. That was all he would have to remember her by.

The site of the henge in the distance turned his stomach. Never would he have suspected feeling that way at the sight of the group of stones. He wondered if he would ever be able to look at them the same way again.

Or if he would ever stop hating them for giving him nothing more than a glimpse of what life could be, then taking it away.

Kaden dismounted before breaking through the tree line, careful to keep watch for any who might be observing, then helped Anna from the saddle. Aidan did the same, swinging his leg over the horse's head and jumping to the ground. Yet to his dismay, Piper refused his assistance, turning her face away and deliberately ignoring him even if it meant scrambling her way out of the saddle.

Kaden was saying goodbye to his mother, so Aidan took

the opportunity to take hold of Piper and pull her aside. He could not allow things to end this way. He would curse himself until his dying day if he did.

"Let go of me," she hissed through clenched teeth, her eyes flashing fire as she glared up at him.

"Not until ye hear what I have to say," he whispered, glancing out to make certain they were not being watched.

"What? Are you going to tell me you wish things didn't have to be this way? That you'll miss me? Big deal. That doesn't do me much good, does it?"

He had hurt her terribly. He'd never heard such disgust in her voice, even when she was at her angriest. He detested himself for it. "I never wanted to hurt ye, nor do I wish to hurt ye now. I wish for nothing more than for this to all resolve itself somehow. Ye have no idea how I wish it."

The warmth of the sun on the back of his neck reminded him of the seer's warning. He would need Isla's ministrations before the sun rose again. The amount of work she had done the night before told him his wound would be grievous, indeed.

He did wish he had asked precisely what was supposed to happen to him. Between worry over Piper and questioning himself as to what might befall him, he's scarcely slept.

He wished to share none of this with Piper, as she might not wish to leave if she knew. He would spare her that, he would do everything in his power to spare her.

With this in mind, there was little time to spare. "I only wished to tell ye how sorry I am. That is all. I care for ye a great deal, and I will never forget how kind ye were to me. Some things are not meant to be."

"Yeah, I know. You don't have to tell me, okay? Please, just let me go." She wouldn't look at him, staring at the ground instead. A single tear fell from one of her downcast eyes, revealing the depth of her pain.

He ran a finger down her cheek, drying the trail of wetness before tilting her chin upward. "I will never regret meeting ye, lass," he whispered when their eyes met. Hers were red, watering, but still hard and hateful. He deserved that, and probably much more.

"I hate you," she whispered before another tear fell, then another, from those dark, scornful eyes.

He deserved that as well. He should never have kissed her, for it only made saying goodbye that much worse. "I hope one day ye can forgive my weakness," he murmured before doing the thing that pained him worst of all.

He let go of her and stepped away, giving her space. She wiped her eyes with the sleeves of her garment before stepping out from behind the tree and walking over to Anna. The two of them exchanged a few murmured words, after which Anna cast him a look of regret over Piper's shoulder.

He pretended not to notice. The last thing he wished was to be an object of pity.

"I guess we better get going," Anna murmured.

"Yeah, I can't wait to get home." Piper bounced up and down on the balls of her feet, filled with energy. Eager, terribly so. He told himself not to take this as a slight upon him, but it was difficult not to do so.

Kaden looked up and down the road and waved them out from inside the tree line once he was certain they would not be seen. "Hurry," he whispered, waving an arm and taking Anna's hand when she joined him.

He turned to his mother. "I do wish ye would join us," he said, and this came as no surprise to Aidan. Naturally, he would wish to secure his mother's safety, and she would be safer in the future. Women were not put to death for witchcraft in Piper's time, which might have been the only thing he could use as an argument in favor of the future.

"What is to be, will be," was all Isla would offer in return. "Ye need not worry so, my son."

"I shall always worry for ye," he muttered, drawing her into a tight embrace before releasing her again.

Aidan stood beside her, watching the trio as they gathered beside the center stone. His heart lodged itself firmly in his throat as he watched his love—his love!—preparing to leave him forever. How could she do this?

How could she not? She had no other choice. She did not love him, not the way he loved her, and as such there was no reason for her to stay.

"Say something to her, man." Isla drove an elbow into his ribs, her voice tight with impatience. "Dinna allow her to leave this way."

"I have tried," he whispered.

"Not hard enough," she admonished him.

"She does not wish to be with me. She longs to be home. I canna hold her back, for that is not what love is. Tis wishing for the best for the other, not for what is best for ourselves."

She wrapped an arm around his, resting her head against his shoulder. "Ye possess more wisdom than I give ye credit for," she murmured softly.

Kaden dug the rune from the pouch hanging from his belt and clenched it in his fist. He looked out over the fields which lay beyond the henge as if taking it all in one final time before leaving it behind forever.

Aidan resolved to commit him to memory, him and Piper both. Even Anna, who seemed to be a decent sort and perhaps the only woman he found worthy of his cousin. The three of them would live only in his thoughts after that, just as he would live in theirs.

A look of surprise crossed Kaden's face as he gazed out over the field.

Then, surprised turned to understanding.

Then, to horror.

Two things happened at once. Aidan heard the pounding of hooves nearby, only moments before at least a hundred men came out from around the bend in the road leading to the village.

And Kaden announced in a tight voice, "Clan Fraser is on the march."

23

"Wait, what?" Anna's head snapped back and forth, glancing out over the field before looking down the road. "Oh, my God! It's not supposed to happen yet!"

"What? What isn't supposed to happen yet?" Piper demanded. They were only moments away from going into the future, and something just had to go wrong. "What's happening?"

Aidan joined them, along with Isla. "How much time passed between Anna's arrival and the battle?" Kaden demanded, staring at his cousin

"A week, at the very least! We haven't been here a week!"

"Time is different," Isla reminded them. "Things have changed. Something might have gone differently this time than it did the last time you went through this. Perhaps they were already closer by the time ye came through."

Kaden curled his hand into a fist and punched the standing stone hard enough that both Piper and Anna gasped. "I didna pay attention! I assumed everything was to be the same! I never thought to ask anyone where the clan was coming from this time. How close they already were. Damn me for a fool!"

Piper was starting to understand, and understanding sure didn't make her feel any better. "What are we supposed to do?" She asked, barely able to breathe as men on horseback bore down on them.

She was asking Kaden, but it was Aidan who answered. "I dinna think there is anything we can do now," he admitted. "They have already seen ye."

Yes, they had already seen her, and her bright red hair. And the tattoos on Anna's arms, visible thanks to her short-sleeved shirt. She had wrapped a hoodie around her waist, unfortunately.

But it wasn't either of the two of them who the rider at the front of the line noticed first. His red hair was just barely brighter than the flush of his cheeks. Had he been drinking, or was he always flushed like that? Maybe it was knowing they were about to ride into battle.

His eyes were cold. Hard. His thin mouth curved up in a smirk. "My, I was led to believe ye had taken your leave of us long ago," the man sneered down at Isla. "Why would I believe such a thing? Who did I hear that from?"

"Ye heard from me, and well ye know it." A man who looked a lot like Aidan rode just behind the first man, and it was he who spoke. Tall, broad-shouldered, with graying brown hair. The eyes were just the same. Hazel, deep-set, and burning.

The man laughed. "I dinna know why I should be surprised. One woman coming to the defense of another."

"I will not have ye speak to my father that way!"

To Piper's horror, Aidan drew his sword and aimed it at the man who sat sneering down from his horse. This could only be Kirk McGregor, someone she had already heard a lot about and hoped she would never meet.

He turned his attention to her and Anna. "Take these women," he announced to no one in particular, and before she knew it several men on foot encircled them.

"Ye will not harm them!" Kaden roared, drawing his sword as Aidan had. Anna let out a choked cry, but Isla shook her head without making a sound.

"Tis not for ye to say!" Kirk snapped back. "And where have ye been these last days, I might ask? When ye knew we were under attack! Your men needed ye, yet ye were consorting with witches!"

Even in the middle of the worst terror she had ever known, Piper knew Kaden's death sentence had pretty much been passed. His chieftain had just announced that he consorted with witches, which was a crime punishable by death.

Just as it was a crime to be a witch.

"Ye will fight by our sides," Kirk ordered. "And if we are victorious, I may consider not reporting ye to the authorities for your crimes."

Both men carried their swords, so it wasn't like they were walking into battle unharmed, but the entire thing filled Piper with dread. They could have been carrying rocket launchers, and her stomach would still turn at the thought of them fighting.

"Remember, they won before," Anna assured her in a

whisper, her eyes moving back and forth over the man who surrounded them.

"Yeah, but things are different now. Remember?" Maybe she shouldn't have said it, but it might've been better for Anna to look at things honestly than for her to fool herself into thinking everything would be okay.

There was definitely a chance everything would not be okay. Just like there was a chance these terrible, filthy men with their dirty hands and their nose-wrinkling stench would kill them in the blink of an eye.

There had been no time for them to go through, Piper understood this. It would have been death for Isla and Aidan if they were left behind, watching three people disappear. They would still have been killed for consorting with witches, and Piper never could have lived with herself if she knew that was true.

Even now, she watched Aidan, unable to breathe when she imagined him fighting out there in hand-to-hand combat with those men. He might still die, and now, she would have to watch.

Kaden was clearly not making his decision quickly enough, since Kirk practically roared. "Make up yer mind! Fight with us now as yer chieftain demands, or I will execute these three witches on the spot. I shall take yer mam first."

"Ye will do no such thing," Aidan warned. He was a different man now. The gentleness and kindness she'd come to love about him were gone. In their place was a steely resolve, a glint in his eye and a sharp edge to his voice. She pitied the man who thought he could fight with him and win.

Her heart swelled with pride even though she knew it was a mistake. It was a mistake for her care for him, and she had walked into it with her eyes open.

And now, she had to watch him fight. He might die. She would have to watch that, too. Without ever telling him she didn't really hate him at all.

And she might die in this time, at the hands of the maniac who shouted orders to his men in preparation for battle while always keeping an eye on his new prisoners. He could easily kill all three of them, and no one would call him into question.

Kaden! He had the rune, didn't he?

While the men argued and Kirk sputtered and spat, her eyes swept the ground. Maybe, just maybe…

"What are ye doing there?" one of the armed men barked at her just before she straightened up from a crouch.

"Nothing," she spat back, practically growling at him until he turned around.

In her clenched fist was the rune which Kaden had been smart enough to drop on the ground. He had known none of the others would see its value, but because he loved Anna, he wanted to be sure she had a way out of this.

This was confirmed when he glanced over at the three of them, questions in his eyes. She nodded, her eyes darting over to the standing stone, and she recognized relief when she saw it. It occurred to her that he didn't care what happened to him so long as Anna was safe.

And when he murmured something to Aidan, and Aidan looked at her, she knew he felt the same way about her.

And, oh, God, she loved him. And he would never know. She couldn't exactly scream it out now, for everyone to hear. They would kill him on the spot, and her alongside him.

She was such an idiot! She could have been smarter, she could've told him before. She could've admitted that all that upset her was knowing he didn't want to come with her, that she wasn't enough for him.

Now, she would never get the chance, and all she could do was blame herself for the rest of her life for watching, helpless, as he strode into battle without even a shield to protect himself.

Kirk smiled at them in a sickening sort of way, the way a person would smile when they were about to hurt somebody. A nasty smile, but one which held delight just the same. "Now that I have three witches here, ye need not fear going into battle against Clan Fraser. They will do their witchcraft for us, will they not? Otherwise, the two of you will be dead by my sword while they watch."

No wonder Kaden had killed him the first time.

Anna stepped forward. "We will do what we can. Do not harm those men. If you harm any of us, we will be of no use to you." Of course, she had been through this before, and she knew how to handle him.

He seemed impressed by this. At least, it shut him up, which was a start.

Piper looked to Isla, who had been silent the entire time. "If you know of any way to help them, now would be the time," she whispered.

"This is going to be pretty shocking," Anna whispered to Piper. "But you can't look away. You have to make it look like you're doing something to help them. Like you're concentrating or something, I don't know. But do not look away, no matter what you do. Don't react. Do you understand?"

One of those things, she knew she could do without breaking a sweat. There was no way she could have pulled her eyes away from the battlefield if she tried, knowing Aidan was out there. She would be watching him the entire time.

If she could do it without reacting, that would be nothing short of a miracle.

The men went into what she guessed was some sort of formation, standing in long lines one after the other. Men on horseback, archers, men on foot carrying shields and swords. Again, the fact that neither Kaden or Aidan carried a shield chilled to the bone. This could not possibly end well.

Like she was reading her thoughts, Isla took Piper's hand. "It will all be as it was meant to be," she murmured. She took Anna's hand in her other hand, repeating herself. *It will all be as it was meant to be.*

Sure. But what was meant to be? And why did she have to be here to watch it?

24

———

"Where have ye been, son?" his father asked as he took his place at his side.

"Ye wouldn't believe me if I told ye," Aidan admitted.

He understood it all now. He knew what was to become of him, what the seer had meant to tell him the day before. He would fall during battle, and Isla would treat his wounds. Whether she would be successful was unknown to him, and perhaps that was the way it ought to be. No man should know when his time was coming.

For he was not carrying his shield, not as he had been before. The shield which had saved his life during the first battle. It would do him no good now. He could only hope his skills were enough to defend himself without it.

For it was not only his life which hung in the balance. It was hers. She would be watching this, she would see him fall.

Would that he might have one last look at her before they began. Would that he might have gotten the chance to tell her what she meant to him, and that perhaps it had been pride all along which kept him from accepting her invitation to join her in the future.

For now, with his life perhaps close to its end, everything was clear. How unfair that was. Only now when there could be no going back to change a single thing did he know what he ought to have said and done.

He ought to have declared his love. He ought to have taken her invitation in the spirit in which she had intended it. She had not merely asked him to join them as a courtesy. She'd been asking something far more, but he had been too great a fool to see it.

All of this and so much more ran through his mind. The taste of her lips, the feel of her body, the softness of her skin and hair, the sweetness of her heart. All she had suffered in life had not been enough to harden her against the world.

Rather than turning her back on him that first night, as would have been well within the lass's rights, she had gone out of her way to spare him what might have been worse than any nightmare.

He was not a praying man, but he prayed then that she would find peace and comfort, that her world would not cause her more pain. That she would find happiness and success in her endeavors.

The Fraser clan stood in the open field, waiting. Kaden stood a few men apart from him and did what he could do issue orders to the men near enough to hear. "When I call for shields, crouch with shields covering your heads," he called out. "Archers, when ye see the shields covering us, fire your arrows."

Aidan did what he could to spread the word of this, as did his father, but there was too much activity, too much chatter, and a great deal of uneasiness thanks to Kirk's unfortunate discovery of the three women.

Did the men trust Kaden any longer? Perhaps they would not listen.

"Attack!" Kirk shouted at the top of his lungs.

A cry rose up from the men. From Aidan and Kaden, too. All of them raced down the slope and across the field, swords at the ready.

He could not think of her. Not now. She would only slow him, dull his instincts.

So many things pressed in on his awareness in those moments. The blue of the sky, the sort of blue he had once gaze up at while lying on his back in this very field as a lad. The sweetness of the air. The lush thickness of the grass beneath his feet, grass which would soon be soaked in blood.

The screams of men who need not be the enemy, charging upon all of them.

They collided in a fury of grunts and screams and curses, a flurry of slashing swords which reflected the sun before they became streaked with blood.

Aidan's sword swung in a wide arc, slashing through the tunic of the man before him. The man turned, hands pressed to his gushing wound, and Aidan ran him through out of mercy before turning to face another foe.

They locked swords, faces mere inches from each other. The man snarled, his jaws snapping as if he thirsted for blood. Aidan raised one foot and kicked out, throwing the man backward. He cried out in rage before charging, and running straight into the end of Aidan's sword, which now wore the blood of two men.

Aidan kicked him away again, leaving him on his knees and turning away before the man fell to the ground. He ducked a flying body. Whose body, whose side, he did not know, then leaped out of the way of a charging, terrified horse with an empty saddle. The animal sent great chunks of bloody mud into the air as it fled the battle.

Kaden was nearby, fighting off two men at once. Aidan joined him, engaging one of them that his cousin need not be outnumbered.

She was watching. She was watching.

No, he could not think of her now.

Yet just as the man he fought fell back, clutching a wound to his throat, he could not help but look back. Up toward the top of the slope, to the henge where Piper waited. Watching.

"Aidan!" Kaden roared, snapping him back to his senses.

Just in time for him to see the sword bearing straight down upon him.

Reflex took over for conscious movement, and perhaps it was for the best that it did. He raised his arm as if he held a shield, crouching as if to duck behind the wooden disk.

Though there was no wooden disk to be had, he managed to keep the sword from cleaving his skull in two.

However, it sliced its way down his arm from elbow to shoulder.

He barely had time to register the pain before Kaden felled the man as one would fell a tree. He would have thanked his cousin were there time to do so.

Retreat sounded, and he realized only vaguely that it was the Frasers who called for it. Sure enough, handfuls of men ran from the field of battle, some of them clutching wounds which slowed them terribly.

His clansmen roared in victory, far fewer of them now dead on the ground and those wounded appearing to be nothing more than inconvenienced. There was a great deal of cheering, celebration, the name MacGregor rising up into the air.

Yet he was dying. He felt his life slipping away, the blood pouring from a wound he could not manage.

This was it. This was how he was meant to die. And in front of her, no less.

He looked back again, knowing he would never regret looking her way in that last moment. For he had been looking toward love and away from the blood and agony all around him.

He had to see her one last time. He had to hear her voice before his eyes closed forever. As some of the men began returning to the henge, so did he. One plodding step at a time, doing what he could to hold a hand over his wound.

It was no use. Blood poured from around his fingers. His life was ending, one moment at a time it slipped away.

He recalled their kiss. One kiss was all he would be afforded. He took another step, then another.

The clan had been victorious, and his father had lived through the battle. As had Kaden. It was not all a loss. Another step, slower now. The world began to take on a gray color, images swimming before him and mixing with memory.

He reached the slope and heard Piper calling for him. If only he had the strength to call out to her, to cry out his love. He could not find his voice. Even that had been taken from him in these last minutes.

He would not give up. Not until he saw her dear, sweet face. He would whisper of his love if need be, but he had to tell her. He could not die without telling her.

His vision doubled as he staggered up the slope, dragging his feet as if they were boulders. He could scarcely move them, their weight growing with each step.

He could not stop. He had to reach her.

His body had other ideas. He fell to his knees before he reached the top of the slope, where the standing stones stood in their semicircle and looked down upon his dying form. Though they could not speak or feel, there was no escaping the sense of their awareness of all that took place.

"Piper—" he managed to gasp before collapsing in the dirt.

The sound of her screams was the last thing he heard before the world went black.

25

"Aidan!" Piper threw herself against the two men standing in front of her, breaking them apart before running down the slope.

"Stop her!" Kirk screamed, but no one seemed particularly interested in what he had to say. His men had just fought a battle and won, and he was still screaming at them.

It didn't matter what he said or what he thought. All that mattered was Aidan, and he was dead. He had to be. Nobody could lose the amount of blood he did and live.

She rolled him over onto his back, which was roughly what she would imagine rolling a horse over would be like. He was so big, all over. She managed it, and he flopped onto his back with a soft groan.

He was alive! Her heart sang. She leaned over him, brushing the dirt from his face. "Please, wake up. Wake up, Aidan. Please, don't leave me. I was so wrong. Please, please don't go."

He didn't hear a word she said, not even flinching when she patted his cheeks. It brought to mind the night they met, and how she tried to wake him from unconsciousness. Only then he had been sick from time travel.

Now, he had a gash running down his arm that had already bled buckets.

She looked up, barely able to see through the tears in her eyes. "Somebody has to help him!"

Yet nobody made a move. They stood there, staring down at her, the men now holding Anna and Isla in place. They were smarter now, and they would not let the other two through so easily. Anna wept openly, struggling against the strong hands holding her.

Isla, meanwhile, stood as still as a statue.

"Is this how you treat one of your clansmen!" Piper demanded, screaming at the top of her lungs. "He fought for Clan MacGregor, and he helped you win! And you would leave him here to die in the dirt! Not one of you is worthy of the air you breathe. And none of you is half as good a man as he is, or as Kaden MacGregor is."

Kaden found her then, falling to his knees beside his cousin. "He is in grievous danger," he muttered, like Piper needed to be told.

She looked up at him, into his blood- and dirt-covered face. "What am I supposed to do?" she asked, desperate for answers while she pressed her hands against the seeping wound. "He's dying. We can't leave him here. Somebody has to help him."

He got to his feet, which didn't seem such an easy thing to do. He had fought like hell out there, so it didn't come as a surprise that he was weak and sore and wounded.

"Someone must see to my cousin!" he demanded. "Let the women through. They may have something which will heal him."

Kirk looked like he might explode, his face almost purple as he turned to the men holding Anna and Isla. "Nay! Ye will not! Tis I who gives orders in this clan, not this man. He has consorted with witches! His own mother is a witch!"

"Enough of this!"

All of them looked in surprise as a bloodied Clyde MacGregor dragged himself up the slope, his eyes fixed on Kirk who still sat in the saddle after having watched the battle rather than participating in it. "I have listened to ye for far too long, Kirk MacGregor. I have allowed ye to speak to me as no man ought to allow another man to speak. And why have I done so?"

"Why?" Kirk laughed. "Because ye have not the courage a man ought to have? Because ye would rather allow me to speak to ye that way than fight back as a man would fight?"

It was clear from some of the mutterings around him that the men did not agree with this. Several of them spat upon the ground, and Piper wondered if Kirk noticed. None of them are very happy with him right now, it would seem. Especially knowing that he would leave one of his men dying on the ground and refuse to help him.

Piper looked down at him, doing everything she could to stop the bleeding in his arm. She removed her babushka, tying it around the wound as tight she could. It seemed like that helped, but he would need to be cleaned and stitched for sure. None of that could happen while he was lying out here.

Clyde leaned on his sword, the tip wedged into the ground. "Nay. I did it for the clan. I have tried every day since ye were named chieftain to help ye understand the folly of yer recklessness. We lost men out there today, and for what? Because ye would not speak to Malcolm Fraser as a man. What good has it done ye? Aye, we defended this land, but for how long? How long will it be before Malcolm Fraser returns with even more men, perhaps from other clans?"

He looked down to where his son lay dying, his voice caught for a second. He pushed that aside, and he sounded stronger than before when he continued. "And now, ye leave him to die after he fought valiantly for ye. For this clan. This tells me ye care not for the people of the clan but rather for yourself! Ye care not for those with whom ye have been entrusted. Ye care only for yourself, just as ye always have."

Kirk seemed at a loss for a second, sputtering as he searched for a cutting retort. "He was seen with witches!"

"He is the son of yer sister." Clyde let this sink in, looking around. "And ye would let him die, why? Because he was in the presence of a witch? Even though he fought as he did, ye would still allow him to die for that? What sort of man are ye, if ye are a man at all?"

With a roar, Kirk lunged out of the saddle and rushed Clyde, drawing his sword as he did. "No man speaks to me that way!" he bellowed, swinging the blade through the air as he charged down the hill.

Clyde did not swing back, but instead ducked the arc of the sword and threw himself against Kirk, knocking him to the ground.

One of the men cried out, and before she knew it a shield was flying through the air. Clyde picked it up, not having the chance to thank the man who had thrown it before having to use it to block another of Kirk's blows, and another. Piper winced every time the sword struck the wooden shield, scarring the wood badly.

"Fight me like a man!" Kirk demanded, swinging the sword, again and again, his fury growing with each blow. He was just a bully, nothing more than a bully. He wanted Clyde to react with rage just as he was doing.

But that was not Clyde's way, and it never had been. Kirk would never understand that. Clyde pushed Kirk down again, and this time he kicked the sword from his chieftain's hand. Finally, he used his own sword, but instead of striking a death blow—it seemed to Piper that he had every right to do it—he only held the tip to Kirk's throat to keep him in place.

"This man cares nothing for any of us," he called out, a little winded but in much better shape than the man on the ground, who was red-faced and sweating like a pig after his exertion. "He does not deserve to sit at the head of our clan, and he never has. I will not kill him, as he is chieftain and 'tis not my place, but I will tell ye now that I believe we ought to have a new chieftain. One who will not allow his men to die after they have fought bravely on behalf of his clan. One who will not act out of spite or bitterness, one who will not insult and degrade his men. One who will not lead us into battle when he might first speak for peace so as to spare the lives of valuable men."

Oh, how Piper wished Aidan could see this. He would

be so proud. She was proud of Clyde, and she had never met him before that day.

One of the men guarding Anna and Isla stepped aside, letting them run down the hill to help Aidan. "Untie the cloth," Isla murmured, pulling one of the little pouches from her belt. Piper had noticed it before, all of them hidden under the cloak she wore.

"Will he live?" Piper whispered with her heart in her throat.

"That remains to be seen, child, but I believe he will. It has been foretold."

"Foretold," Anna whispered, looking to Piper.

"Aye. Elspeth told me. Tis why I made certain to have enough of this in my possession when we came today. I knew what was to happen, but I could not speak of it."

Piper thought her head might explode. "You should've told us!" she hissed.

She slowly shook her head as she spread the mixture of herbs over Aidan's wound. "Nay, I could not. To speak of it would mean changing the course of fate. Those who see are not permitted to speak of it unless—"she shook her head, "—even then, we are not permitted to reveal anything that might protect even those we love. There are times in which it feels like a curse." She stroked Aidan's forehead before continuing.

Piper couldn't argue with that. She wanted to slap Isla across the face for keeping this to herself, but the woman made a point. If it couldn't be done, it couldn't be done. All she could do was prepare herself and join the group on their way to the henge, so she could help Aidan in every way she could.

Anna looked up at Piper. "You know we can't leave him here, right?" she whispered, glancing up at the standing stone. "They might not take care of him. He needs to be cleaned up, and they probably won't do a good job of it."

Isla nodded. "I must agree. His wound will be left to fester without the skill of either one such as myself or someone with more knowledge than myself, and that person does not exist in the village. I know this."

"We have to take him with us. There's no other way." Piper stroked his forehead, which was so hot and sweaty. He would get a fever soon, she knew he would, once his wound became infected. He would be lucky if he managed to only have his arm chopped off.

But that would kill him, too. Death would be more of a mercy for a man like him than a lifetime of walking around with only one arm.

Kaden joined them, holding Anna as he watched his mother work on Aidan. She tied the cloth tight around his arm again while Anna whispered what they had just been talking about.

Piper looked over his shoulder to find the guards who'd been holding her back now taking Kirk by the arms and leading him away. The men cheered, rushing to Clyde and announcing him the clan chieftain. "Oh, my God," she whispered with a smile. Yes, Aidan would want to see this.

"Is it that easy?" Anna asked when she realized what was going on. "Can they just declare him chieftain and that's it? There's no election or anything?"

Kaden offered a tired little laugh. "Nay, my love. The chieftain is chosen, either by the former chieftain before he dies or by the men once they decide they have found their chieftain. I have no doubt after what happened today, he has their support, and perhaps he always did but they were too afraid to speak aloud. Now, watching Kirk try to murder him and seeing how Clyde refused to fight back, that is all they need. They have every reason in the world to turn their backs on Kirk turned toward a much better choice."

Even though he was exhausted, there was unmistakable pride in Kaden's voice. Piper found herself glad he could witness this before they went back.

He was frowning when he looked down at his cousin. "He will not be glad to return with us," he mused. "Does he need a doctor's care?"

Isla shook her head, though the question might not have been strictly directed at her. "He verra well might, though we might do much to prevent that. Unless he develops a fever, he ought to survive and recover well. He is a strong lad, and while the wound is deep it did not tear through much of the tissue at once, merely striking an artery. We will need to burn the would closed, perhaps, but it will need to be cleaned before we do."

"We?" Kaden asked.

"Aye. We. Certainly, I canna allow ye to take him now, when I will not know what became of him. I shall have to come along with ye."

She looked up at her son, a smile now breaking over her face. "As I said, what is to be will be. And the future is much kinder to those such as myself."

Clyde joined them, falling to his knees at Aidan's side. "How is he?" he asked, looking at the blood-soaked cloth covering his wound.

There was only one person who could explain things,

and even she wouldn't know where to start. But they didn't have much time. She had to make it short and sweet.

She extended a bloody hand, but then his hand was bloody, too. "My name is Piper Kaminski, and I love your son very much. I know he would be proud of you."

He raised a skeptical brow but took her hand, anyway. "Tis glad I am to meet ye… I believe."

"He's very badly wounded, as you can see," she explained. "And I know it'll be impossible for you to understand this, but you have to believe me. I only want what's best for him. I—we—can take him someplace where he'll be in much better care than he could be here. I can't stay to take care of him because I'll be called a witch and that will get you in trouble for harboring me, but—I don't mean any offense—you all might not have the skill to keep him clean and cared for. You don't have the medicines he'll need if he develops a fever and his wound festers and poisons his blood. Do you see what I mean?"

"Aye. I believe I do. Where would ye take him?"

"I am so sorry to tell you this, but it's someplace you could never go to."

"Ye could, perhaps," Kaden mused. "But once ye return, things would not be the same." He was right. Clyde might walk back into a world where Kirk was still chieftain and the battle with the Frasers was still waiting to be fought. That would be a huge step in the wrong direction.

"I canna make sense of what ye are telling me," Clyde confessed.

Kaden clasped his arms when he stood. "Uncle. Ye have always been like a father to me. I thank ye for that and for all ye have sacrificed for me. I know ye love your son."

"More than myself," Clyde admitted, his voice thick with emotion.

"He might verra well die if he is not seen to, but that will mean taking him away with us. If ye wish for him to live, ye must let him go now."

Clyde barely held back tears as he reached down to pat his son's shoulder. "I do love ye, lad," he whispered. "As does yer mam. Ye made me terribly proud today, but ye always have since the day ye came into the world."

He looked to Kaden again. "Do as ye will. Take care of him, man."

"I will that," Kaden vowed before lifting Aidan and throwing him over his shoulder. Piper winced, reaching out like she could've done anything to help. She couldn't stop herself. That was the man she loved.

"We had better hurry," Anna whispered, taking Piper and Isla by the hand. "Come on. Clyde, sir, you'd better go away now and pretend you never saw any of this."

The poor guy was completely baffled. "I will," he grunted, turning away. Every line of his body reflected the tension, the struggle to leave his son behind. But he walked away just the same. Piper thought she had never seen anything so heroic.

"Hurry," Piper urged, knowing Aidan had little time now. They made it to the top of the slope and stood before the center stone. Most of the men had started returning to the village by now, probably happy to be finished with the battle and glad to have a new chieftain. She hoped their exhaustion and exhilaration would be enough to keep them from paying attention to what was about to happen.

She held Anna's hand, waiting for everybody else to link hands before touching the rune to the center stone.

She wasn't afraid anymore. Not for herself. Not when she had someone much more important to worry about.

The rune glowed from between her clenched fingers, and she closed her eyes and waited for that rush of air…

26

He was on fire. The entire world was on fire.

He was barely able to open his eyes, though he struggled to do so.

Was that Piper swimming above him? No, it could not be. He imagined her. Nothing more.

For no one could exist in this hellish place where all was hot, so hot, burning through his skin and muscle and bones, through his head.

He deserved this suffering. He had killed men the very day of his death and had no time to repent. This was the punishment he would suffer for all eternity. Lying in a pool of his own sweat while his body burned and there was no way to cry out for help and no one to help him even if he could.

He sank deeper, deeper, into the darkness where there was no pain. A blessed relief, indeed.

When his eyes opened, it was dark. And cool. So very cool. And comfortable. There was something beneath his head. Something covered him as well—his hands slid along its surface, but barely. He could scarcely move.

What had become of him? He did not recognize his surroundings. This was not his parents' home, nor was it Isla's cottage.

If this was Hell, it was very comfortable at the moment. Surprisingly so.

"Aidan?" A familiar whisper, a rustling across the room. A weight on the bed, pressing it down.

He turned his head to the side to find the one face he had never expected to see again. In the darkness, her bright-red hair was not so bright, yet he recognized it just the same.

His lips were parched, cracked, and he ran his tongue along them before mouthing her name. *Piper.* Was she here in hell with him? No, she did not deserve anything of the sort.

He doubted he deserved heaven, so she was not an angel.

Which meant he had lived.

She lifted one of his hands and pressed her forehead to it, trembling. "You had a very, very close call," she sighed. "So close. I thought we lost you more than once. You were so sick."

Sick? "What—" he managed to gasp.

"Don't tire yourself. You have to rest. I'll explain as much as I can." She kissed his hand again and again. "I thought you were gone forever. I thought this was all for nothing."

What was for nothing? He did wish she would get on

with telling him what he had missed, since she said she would.

"I'm sorry if you're not happy about this—and I totally understand if you aren't—but we had to bring you back here. I know, it's a hassle. Worse than a hassle. But Isla said if we left you back there, you would die. And now that I've seen what you went through I know you would. You soaked through the bedding in hours. Hours. Over and over, sweating and burning up, then shaking with the worst chills I've ever seen. Convulsing sometimes. The best Isla could say was there had to be blood on the sword that struck you, and it poisoned you somehow. I mean, that's the most scientific she could get. But between that and the dirt that probably got into the wound, the amount of blood you lost wasn't even the worst of it."

She shivered. "What she brought with her could only do so much. It was keeping the blood poisoning from spreading, but it wasn't stopping it. Just slowing it down. So Anna reached out to the executives who hope to sign us and explained that I was really sick and needed antibiotics but didn't have the money on me to go to the hospital. I'm not sure I wanna know how they got their hands on the drugs, but they did it. I guess they wanna sign us pretty badly. And we probably don't have a choice but to go along with them now, not like I had a problem with the idea in the first place."

She shook her head, waving a hand. "Anyway. I'm getting off-track. Once we started giving you the drugs, you turned around really fast. It was like a miracle. You never would've made it if we left you there. Please, you've gotta believe me. Kaden and Anna and Isla will tell you the same thing when you see them."

He tried to take all of this in, but it was a struggle with his head in such a state. Little wonder he felt so weak, so exhausted and confused. And hungry. He had a powerful hunger.

"How long?" he whispered.

"Six days. This is day seven. This is the first time you've woken up and been anything close to coherent. Anna had to leave this morning. She took Isla and Kaden with her."

This came as the biggest surprise of all. His eyes widened, and she nodded in understanding. "Yes. It was a big deal. But your fever broke overnight, and it seemed like you were getting better, and she had to get back home to her dad. We were never supposed to be here this long. The production company agreed to foot the bill for the hotel as long as I said I needed it. Since I was supposed to be sick, you know. It took a lot of convincing to get Kaden to leave you. He didn't want to. He's really stubborn, isn't he?"

Aidan nodded. Kaden had gotten aboard one of the airplanes, the birds in the sky which allowed men and women to fly as if they had wings.

"I'm so sorry," she winced. "I know you didn't wanna come back here, and I wouldn't have brought you if it wasn't for how sick you were. Isla knew you needed more than what could be done for you in the village. There weren't antibiotics back then, of course, and she couldn't hang around the village and take care of you. I mean, even with your dad being the chieftain now—that could get him into trouble, and she didn't want to do that to him."

The chieftain.

The chieftain?

The chieftain!

When he tried to sit up, the room spun. Piper eased him back against the pillow. "Not so fast, big guy. I know, it's a shock to you. I wish you could've seen him. It was incredible, Aidan. He was so brave." She explained in great detail how his father had stood up to Kirk, even going so far as to get up from the bed and move about the room, pretending to be one man and the other in turn.

"And then the men took Kirk away and cheered for your dad, and they said he was the new chieftain. I was so proud of him for you," she whispered, hands clasped over her breast. "I wished you could see it. I tried to remember as much of it as I could so I could tell you when you woke up."

His father. Chieftain. Finally, he had used the rage boiling in his heart and turned it upon the man.

Yet he had not struck out with his sword. Yes, she must have remembered it correctly, for that was precisely what his father would have done.

The entire thing left him breathless, wondering what had become of his father after that day. How he wished he could have seen it, and that he might have seen the years to come.

His mouth worked, his mouth too parched to allow him to speak. Yet she seemed to understand.

She held up a finger, turning on the light above the desk and straightening a few papers which she carried to the bed and held up for him after turning on the light overhead. "See? I took a little time off from nursing you—they practically threw me out of the room and told me to go outside and get some fresh air, and went to the library. I wanted to know if we changed anything. And we did."

She read aloud from one of the pages. "Under the leadership of Clyde MacGregor, the Battle at the Henge ushered in a new era of peace for not only the MacGregors but for all surrounding clans. Over the seven years in which Clyde MacGregor served as clan chieftain, he secured the boundaries of all clan territories in the surrounding area and sought to form alliances which benefitted all involved."

She looked to him. "And there's a list of all the things he did after that. He served for seven years, and they were the most peaceful years ever. After that, too, for generations. It was all because of him. Because he wanted to talk peace and strategy before going to war. He's a legend, Aidan. There's even a statue dedicated to him near the sight of the battle."

It was not manly to give way to tears in front of a woman, but he supposed allowances could be made when a man had come close to dying. He wept silent tears for all he had lost, and for all his father and his clan had gained. For it had been the sight of his son dying on that slope which had spurred Clyde to speak as he never had before. According to Piper's telling of it, at least.

Piper rested her head on his chest. "I know. I know."

And he knew she did.

Once he managed to get his emotions under control—the act of crying had wiped away what little energy he had—he lifted her head from his chest. "I love ye," he managed to croak, weak and soft.

"I love you," she smiled. "I'm so sorry for everything I said. I never hated you. It killed me out there, knowing I could never tell you how sorry I was and how I was only angry because it seemed like you didn't want me enough."

"I want ye, lass. I want ye most awfully." He stroked her cheeks with his thumbs, soaking in the sight of her. "I was foolish and prideful, trying to send ye away as I did. Telling myself everyone needed me. Tis I who needs ye, lass. It seems my father got on verra well without me."

"It hurt him so badly to send you away," she replied with a catch in her throat and a reddening of her eyes. "He didn't want to. But he knew he had to because he loved you and it was the only way to save you."

Yes, that sounded like the man.

"Are you mad that we brought you back? You can tell me. I can take it."

Mad? "Nay, lassie," he breathed. "Not at all. Ye saved me in every way. Ye are saving me still, remaining here when ye might have gone home with the others."

"Like I would leave you."

"As I would never leave ye, my darling one." He kissed her forehead, her nose, drawing her face closer all the time until their lips met.

This was as close to Heaven as he would ever get, and he knew it.

He would be forever grateful.

"Lord love a Highlander," Piper murmured with a grin as they walked the familiar path through the park to the standing stones. "I've never seen a man recover as quickly as you have, especially when he came close to dying."

"I have far too much to do, and canna see wasting my time in bed," he argued.

"No?" she winked, sliding an arm around his waist. "I thought you liked all our time in bed."

"Aye, and when I have the strength I ought to, I am certain I shall like it a great deal more," he growled before kissing the top of her head. Their days since his awakening had been spent in bed, side-by-side, doing what she referred to as "binge-watching" and eating a great deal of food to get his energy where it needed to be.

The stitching in his arm was still tight, but the wound was healing well. He was close to fully recovering from all he had suffered.

More than anything, there was the certainty that the woman by his side loved him and would be by his side always, showing him the wonders of her world.

Truly, there was more similarity than difference. At the heart of it, people were the same. Selfish at times, hateful and hurtful, but on the whole good and decent. Wishing to come to the aid of others. They loved, and they worked, and they wed and had bairns, and the entire thing repeated itself again. Just as it had so many times over since he had first walked these hills.

The standing stones shone up ahead, the midday light hitting them and turning them nearly white. It seemed they beckoned. And if they could smile, it would be a knowing one. A playful one. For they had watched over him as he had nearly died and watching him now, centuries later.

"We had to pretend you were injured during a role-playing game," Piper explained. "That was the only way we could excuse the way you and Kaden and Isla were dressed.

It turns out lots of people do that sort of thing around here, especially since the battle between you and the Frasers was so pivotal."

He saw it up ahead. The statue she had spoken of. He was nearly afraid to approach it and wondered why. His heart pounded nearly as hard as it had the day of the battle.

"It wasn't here before," she whispered as they took slow steps toward it, sitting beyond the henge and surrounded by flowers and benches where people might sit and rest. "This is totally new in this time."

He barely heard her. There was his father.

Taller than he'd been in reality, and broader in the shoulder. It seemed whoever had described him over time had exaggerated a bit. He was larger than life, and as Piper had described it, a legend. He was holding a sword in one hand and a dove in the other, symbolizing peace. His head held high, a proud look about him.

"Och, Da," Aidan breathed, touching the statue's foot. It was not his father's, but this was the closest he would ever come. "Thank ye for all of it. For showing me that being a man does not always mean raising a fist. For wanting peace. For your patience. Your goodness. Thank ye." He bowed his head, wishing he could speak to the man just once more. "I am proud of ye, so terribly proud."

Piper touched his shoulder, her cheek against his arm. "He did a good job raising you," she observed.

"He showed through example, and a few well-earned thrashings," Aidan chuckled. "I deserved it, and I never made those mistakes again."

"Careful. We don't do that in this time," she teased.

Just another thing he would have to remember.

He kissed his fingers and touched them to the statue once more before turning away. "All is as it should be," he decided, the two of them holding hands as they left the park.

"I think so," Piper agreed with a grin. "But we'll see how you feel about it once we get on that plane tonight."

He heaved a heavy sigh, looking once more over the amphitheater and the stones, knowing his father's statue stood behind him and would remain there for many years. It was time to leave the past behind for good and for all—he would recall those he loved, but there were others he loved in this time.

He stopped, turning to the one he loved best of all and taking her face in his hands. "If ye can manage all ye have done for my sake, I believe I can manage not to make a fool of myself while we fly through the air."

She kissed him, standing on tiptoe to reach. "Good. Now, all we have to do is find out if you get airsick."

"Airsick?"

She giggled, wrapping her arms about his waist before starting off again. "Oh, there are so many things for you to learn about. One of the executives knows someone who knows someone, and we've got papers for you to travel."

Suddenly, something occurred to him which had not before. "What became of the rune?"

"I don't know. Nobody does. I held it in my hand as we were coming through, but when we got here, I wasn't holding it anymore." She lifted her shoulders. "Isla said maybe that was how it was always meant to work. You know how she is."

"Aye, I do," he murmured, casting one last look over his shoulder. "Perhaps the rune's work is not finished."

The stones offered no answer.

They stood there as ever they had, silent and watchful.

Filled with secrets.

Keep reading for an excerpt from the next book in the series!

EXCERPT: LEITH

Book Three of the *Highland Passages* Series!

Melissa's excited. She's got a wedding to plan. Her own. To her fiancé Jimmy, who is in a band. They have the honeymoon tickets. Venice. Woohoo! So, one night she to surprise him with cooking a nice romantic dinner. She's even got a special gift for him. The lucky rune he told her he found in Scotland, she's had mounted and put into a necklace that she's going to present to him tonight.

She didn't plan on catching him in bed with a bimbo.

But she still has the tickets. So, she decides to travel anyway, but she's sure as heck not going to Venice. Plus, she's keeping the cool necklace with the rune. After scanning the availabilities, she becomes entranced with the pictures of Scotland. And she wouldn't mind meeting a sexy Scottish guy so she can forget about the cheater. It would so serve him right if she met a hot Scottish guy. And, hey, she's got a degree in history, and she knows there's some cool stuff to check out there, so she's going. In fact, she's going to the same henge he sent her pictures of. Among many other places.

Leith MacManus, hunky, bearded, Highlander, is a distant cousin of the Frasers on his mother's side. Leith's the firstborn son of laird of the MacManus clan. His father's getting older and wants Leith wed and it's time for his son to marry the one he betrothed him to secretly, ages ago. But—oops!—good old da never told Leith all this time that he made this arrangement. Happens that Leith can't stand Flora MacNeill.

Things change when an odd woman, dressed even more oddly drops into his life.

CHAPTER 1

Melissa took the necklace from the jeweler's hand and held it up to the light to admire the work. "It's beautiful. Just what I had in mind."

The lady let out a little laugh and mimed wiping sweat from her brow. "I'm glad. I wanted to do it justice. It isn't every day somebody finds an old rune."

"He'll love it." Melissa took note of the silver setting, tines shaped like claws holding the rune in place, suspended on a silver chain. "I knew this rune would sit in a drawer someplace if we didn't do something special with it. He says it's good luck."

"Really? How so?"

She stared at the small, black rock. So smooth, like time had worn down its edges. Jimmy said he'd found it by a henge not far from where the band had their stellar performance outside Edinburgh, the performance that led to the band being signed by a record label willing to go all-in on making them stars.

And there she was, engaged to be married to one of those stars. It might mean an entirely new life.

"His band signed a recording contract based off the performance they gave the day before he found it," she explained. "I mean, if that's not good luck, I don't know what is. I figured he'd better wear it around his neck wherever he goes if that's the sort of fortune it brings!"

"You're so right," the jeweler nodded, eyes wide. "I've seen a lot of older pieces—stones, crystals, you know—but this is unique. Did he inquire as to its age?"

Melissa smiled at the thought of her fiancé doing anything like that. "No. Not Jimmy. That's not his way. He's a little superstitious, maybe, but that's as far as he goes. He might say he's going to do something, but something else comes his way to catch his attention, and that's that."

"Shiny Object Syndrome," the jeweler mused with a wry grin.

"You would know," Melissa agreed with a glance around the showroom, and the two of them laughed together.

The cases were filled with other unique pieces—more artwork than jewelry, if one were splitting hairs. Melissa had chosen this artisan in particular because of the nature of her work. She seemed a perfect fit for something as special as this ancient rune.

If it really was ancient. It might have been a piece of junk, something from a gift shop. She had never seen the symbol carved into it before looking it up online. Fehu, it was called. It was supposed to bring money, prosperity— and it had certainly seemed to prove itself. For the first time in his life, Jimmy had a future to look forward to that didn't involve an office filled with cubicles.

The thought of that day job snapped her back to full attention, as the entire point of this excursion was to run her errands before he got home from work. Melissa happily handed over the money for the necklace and thanked the jeweler profusely. "He'll love it," she gushed, shaking her hand. "It's the perfect way to commemorate a new phase in life, isn't it?"

The jeweler agreed, but then, of course, she would. Melissa left the shop with a spring in her step.

What was there to be unhappy about, after all? She was finally going to spend time with her fiancé after being apart for most of the past three weeks. Between two work conferences and the trip to Edinburgh, they'd barely had more than a few minutes together. It might as well have been a lifetime.

She wondered as she walked to the cute little artisan shop a few blocks from the jeweler's how much longer he would stay at his day job now that the band was on its way to something bigger. Selling pharmaceuticals wasn't exactly his passion, but he'd done well enough with it up until then. It had afforded him a nice little apartment in a desirable Chicago neighborhood and enough money to put toward their wedding planning.

But that wasn't enough, nor did she expected to be. Not when a person had a dream, as he did.

If only she could have been there with him in Scotland. It still irked her that she hadn't been able to take time off from work at the museum. From everything he told her, it'd been a stellar experience.

While she'd helped visitors find the nearest restroom. There was that history degree, paying off.

It was with their long-awaited reunion in mind that she picked up a basket at the shop and searched for ingredients to make one of his favorite meals. Fresh fettuccine served with cacio e pepe—cheese and pepper—just like they'd shared in Rome when they first met. She was a history student running around Europe, researching during summer break, while he'd been at his first work conference after accepting a position straight out of college.

For somebody who shredded hard, thumping rock at night and on the weekends, he knew how to put on a suit and tie and pretend to be a professional when he had to.

They would definitely have to revisit that little restaurant on their honeymoon. While the bulk of their time would be spent in Naples, probably her favorite city in Italy, it wouldn't seem right if they didn't revisit the spot where they'd shared their first meal.

A block of Parmigianino Reggiano, a package of fresh pasta, bread and fancy olive oil for dipping. She found a box of dark chocolate truffles for dessert and tucked it in with the rest before heading for the produce section.

It had been a long time since she'd cooked a surprise meal for him, the three years of their relationship having settled them into a rut. That was all going to change. Now that he was home, there was nothing left but to finish planning their wedding and look forward to the rest of their lives together.

She chanced a look at herself in the window outside the shop just as she left and took note of her wide smile. Sunshine caught the golden highlights in her light brown hair, making it shine. Wide, oval sunglasses hid her blue eyes, but she had the feeling that if she could see them, she'd find them full of light. It wasn't every day she got her fiancé back.

And she could hardly wait to give him the necklace. He wasn't typically much for jewelry, but it was unassuming enough that she thought he could at least wear it during gigs. Or maybe it would become part of his everyday wardrobe. She hoped so, hoped he would always wear a symbol of his dream coming true. He'd worked hard and held out hope when a lot of people would've given up.

By the time she reached his building in Lakeview, she was juggling shopping bags and an arm full of fresh tulips while fishing for the key to the apartment in her oversized purse. Her fingers brushed up against the box holding the necklace, giving her a little thrill. Just like she had before taking the stone to the jeweler, there was a funny feeling in the back of her mind of there being more to it than just an old, carved stone.

But that was silly, wasn't it?

The apartment was quiet, just as she expected it to be. Jimmy would be at work, probably stuck in one of a million meetings after the conference and up to his eyeballs in emails. The thought of him coming home to surprise meal and a gift made her smile from ear to ear as she placed the bags on the kitchen counter with a happy sigh.

Soon, this would be her home, and this would be the sort of thing she did for him whenever possible. For her, cooking was a way of showing love, especially on a hectic day.

When the bedroom door opened, breaking the silence, her smile faltered.

"Who's there?" She heard Jimmy's voice a moment

before she saw him walk barefoot into the kitchen, wrapping a towel around his waist. He'd just gotten out of the shower, water beading on his shoulder and chest, his dark hair combed back by his fingers.

For a second, the fact that he was home rather than in the office threw her off-kilter. But then she smiled and held her arms out. "Oh, you ruined my surprise." She pouted, ready for a hug. "Why aren't you still at work? Are you feeling okay?"

Just before she reached him, a noise from inside the bedroom froze her in place.

It wasn't the sort of noise a person just imagined, and it wasn't random noise from another apartment next door or downstairs. It was the sound of the door between the bedroom and the bathroom closing, followed by footsteps.

Her eyes met Jimmy's, and the way his widened in surprise before softening in shame stopped her heart. He knew he was caught. There was no explaining his way out of it.

Especially when a redhead wrapped in a towel padded out into the hall. She was wet, too, long hair dripping on her chest and shoulders.

Jimmy stammered, hands held out in a defensive gesture. "Mel, let me explain—"

He thought there was an explanation. That she needed this spelled out for her like she was a child who couldn't put two and two together.

It was so ridiculous, she burst out laughing before she knew what she was doing. "You're kidding me. You are freaking kidding me! Do you think you can talk your way out of this? I'm your fiancée, James!"

The redhead gasped. "You didn't tell me you were engaged," she hissed, glaring at Jimmy and wrapping her arms around herself like she was embarrassed.

She turned to Melissa, her face a mask of surprise and shame. "I'm so sorry! Seriously, if I'd known—"

Melissa held up her hand, shaking her head. "I don't want to hear it. Honestly." Not when her entire world was falling to pieces around her. Knowing that the girl involved had no idea she existed didn't exactly make things better.

And there he was, looking embarrassed and pained and ashamed. All of which he deserved to feel, no question. "I'm so sorry," he murmured. "Mel, I love you. I'm so sorry."

There went that laughter again, bubbling up from inside her and making its way out of her mouth before she could stop it. It seemed like there was no controlling her reactions, but then again how did a person react to something like this? How was she supposed to react to her world falling apart?

Shock numbed her, and she was glad of it, or else she might've made a fool of herself in front of a naked, dripping stranger and the man she'd only just been fantasizing about spending her life with.

She barely noticed the way her right hand fumbled with her left, working the diamond solitaire off her ring finger before slamming it onto the counter, where it sat with the shopping bags and the flowers she'd intended to put in water. "If you loved me, you wouldn't have done this. Congratulations on the band's success."

Jimmy was frozen in place.

Melissa then looked at the redhead, who was now near tears. "And good luck with him," she spat, pushing her way past Jimmy and practically running for the front door. She managed to escape before he caught her—he wouldn't come chasing after her wearing nothing but a towel, she knew that much.

It was only when she reached the sidewalk outside the building that she realized she couldn't breathe. She leaned against the wall, one hand to her chest, deliberately drawing air into her lungs before forcing it out again. Slowly, as carefully as she could.

What was she supposed to do? What did a person do after having their entire future destroyed? All the plans, all the hopes, the dreams. The fantasies about what life would be like once they were married, all of the happy days they had before them. All of it crushed, because he couldn't keep it in his pants.

How long had he been lying to her? How long had she been a fool? And exactly what else was he doing in Scotland when he wasn't performing on stage?

Her stomach churned as she stumbled to the curb, signaling a taxi to take her home. To think, if she hadn't cut out of work early to pick up the necklace and go to the store, she would have completely missed bumping into Jimmy's little girlfriend. If she'd only waited an hour, she might have been blissfully unaware, thinking her life was completely on track.

What an idiot she was. There must have been signs she'd missed! Weren't there always clues in situations like this? How many times had she told herself girls who'd been cheated on this way must have been willfully ignorant of what was going on right under their noses?

Here she was, one of those girls. Wondering when

everything had gone so wrong. And how she could've missed the whole thing. How long he'd been sleeping around behind her back. How many close calls there might've been. One afternoon of infidelity had set her imagination on fire and cast doubts over the last three years.

It wasn't until she got home that it finally sank in, the shock wearing off. That was when the tears started, falling hot and hard, stealing her breath. She screamed into a pillow, punched her mattress, before curling up in a ball and weeping brokenly.

The wedding. The wedding she'd been planning for six months. It was a good thing that most of it was still only in her head, scattered along Pinterest boards and written down on her phone. Thank goodness she hadn't spent any money yet.

Except for the honeymoon, and the tickets they'd bought to fly to Naples.

It was full dark by the time she crawled out of bed and washed her face, aching all over. The reflection over the sink in her tiny bathroom looked nothing like the girl she'd seen only hours earlier, reflected in the window outside the shop. That girl had been vibrant, excited, her life full of promise. She had something to look forward to, that girl. Marriage, maybe kids if they were lucky. A fiancé whose music career was poised to take off. A honeymoon on the horizon.

Now? Now she had puffy eyes and a frown which tugged downward the corners of her mouth. She had worry lines between her brows and a red, chapped nose from all the tissues she'd used.

What was a girl supposed to do when the world caved in? What was the first step?

Should she call her friends? No, the wound was too fresh. She couldn't go through it all again so soon. Besides, none of them had ever liked Jimmy very much in the first place. Now she understood why, of course, but she was hardly in the right mental state to hear *I told you so*. Not that any of her friends would be that rude, but she would imagine them thinking it just the same.

What else was there?

Within ten minutes, she was seated in front of her laptop with a bottle of wine on the coffee table while she logged into her account with the airline to cancel their tickets. Funny how a tiny voice in the back of her mind asked whether she was jumping the gun by canceling the trip. Even then, even after knowing he had betrayed her in the worst way possible, she still wondered in some tiny part of her heart and mind whether this was the right thing to do.

How ridiculous.

She canceled the tickets, accepting a credit with the airline. What a relief that she had reserved the flight on her credit card, though she now had a choice to make. Should she go someplace on her own? Maybe leave the credit sitting there for a rainy day, so to speak?

Or should she just throw caution to the wind, take some of the money she'd saved up for the wedding, and go on a vacation of her own? She'd been saving all of her time off from the museum for the days leading up to the ceremony and ten days after that, but now?

She wasn't sure she could stomach visiting the entire country of Italy, or even anything too close by. What a shame, the thought that her ex-fiancé had ruined her favorite country. Maybe time would soothe her wounds, but for now, she couldn't bear the thought of being near where they'd met, and where they'd planned to celebrate their marriage.

What about Scotland?

She blinked, staring over the laptop screen and out the window. Wondering at that sudden thought and the impulse behind it. Maybe it was a sense of tit-for-tat, getting back at him by going to the country he'd just left and meeting a hunky Scotsman to have a fling with.

Wouldn't that be perfect? She couldn't manage to make it out there for his gig, but she'd go after he'd broken her heart. The jerk, the coward, the creep.

Besides, it wasn't like she'd never been there. Scotland had always held an interest for her thanks to its henges and standing stones, its mythology.

Yes. That was exactly what she needed. To go someplace where there was plenty of fresh air and gorgeous scenery, someplace she could reconnect with herself and her love of history and the outdoors.

Her gaze wandered to the other item on the coffee table, something she'd pulled from her purse and left lying there as a reminder of the way the night could've gone.

The necklace, nestled in its box.

"What the hell?" she whispered, taking the necklace out and fixing the clasp at the back of her neck. The rune nestled against her chest, where she figured it would stay for a while. No sense in letting something so beautiful go to waste just because of the idiot she'd had it made for.

I hope you enjoyed Aidan!
For more Annis Reid books click here!

Sign up for the newsletter to be notified of new releases.

Click on link for
Newsletter